Their Wicked Forever

A Cunningham Family Novel

EMBER CASEY

You can contact Ember at ember.casey@gmail.com.
Website: http://embercasey.com.

ISBN: 1-5300-4291-7
ISBN-13: 978-1-5300-4291-3

BOOKS BY EMBER CASEY

Want to be the first to know when Ember has a new
release?
Want exclusive extras and freebies?
Join Ember's newsletter!
(http://www.embercasey.com/newsletter.html)

PROLOGUE
LILY

"What's the occasion?" Calder asks.

God, he looks delicious tonight. I might be a little biased, but I'm pretty sure I'm married to the sexiest man in existence. I'm not sure what I like most—those broad shoulders, those dark and devilish eyes, that perfect hint of stubble on his cheeks—but I could eat him up. And that finely cut suit he's wearing definitely completes the picture. I told him he needed to dress up for dinner, but all I can think about is how I want to rip all those clothes right off him. Maybe we should skip dinner. I think I'd much rather push him down on the table and devour *him* instead.

Wow, horny much? Calder has always had a very strong effect on me, but it's particularly distracting tonight. I fight back my more primal urges and slide my hands down the dress I picked out for tonight. It's a gorgeous gown—midnight blue with delicate beading along the low neckline—and this is the first time I've had the chance to wear it. I want to get some use out of it while I can, which means keeping it on through dinner, at the very least. There will be time to devour each other later.

"It's a very special occasion," I tell Calder, leading him over to the table by the window. This room has one of the best views in the entire Cunningham mansion, overlooking the estate's main rose garden—which, incidentally, is where Calder and I had our wedding ceremony this past summer. Though none of the roses are in bloom this time of year, the bushes are lit with twinkling lights that bounce off the thin blanket of snow on the ground. The whole scene is like a winter wonderland, and it's the perfect backdrop for tonight.

I've draped the table with a silver tablecloth and dotted the surface with short candles that flicker as we draw near. Calder raises an eyebrow, apparently skeptical of this mysteriously formal display, but he doesn't say a word as he settles into his seat. Still, I can feel his dark eyes boring into me, and my skin grows warm as I take my seat across from him.

"I thought we might play a little game," I say. Calder has never been able to turn down a game.

He leans forward, his eyes taking on that wicked gleam I know so well. "What sort of game?"

My stomach flutters at the rumble of his voice. Once again I have the overwhelming urge to throw him down on the table and rip off his clothes. I take a moment to spread my napkin across my lap as I try to keep my thoughts under control.

"This game is very simple," I say. "You simply have to guess why we're having this dinner."

His lips curl up. He's intrigued. "What are the

rules?"

"You get ten yes or no questions," I tell him, trying not to notice the way a piece of his dark hair has fallen across his brow. He's normally so polished that somehow even the slightest hint of dishevelment looks sexy on him. I just want to take that little bit of hair around my finger and—

"What are the stakes?" he asks.

Focus, Lily, I tell myself. *You have a game to win.*

"If you can guess why we're here, then you're in charge tonight," I tell him. "I'm yours. For whatever you wish to do."

Before I even finish, I can tell that he's already getting some ideas. He's started to get a hungry sort of look that makes my skin burn even hotter. It'll be a miracle if we make it all the way through dinner—but given our history, I knew that already. I don't think we've ever made it through one of our games without tearing the clothes off of each other. Hell, our entire relationship started as a game. A sexy, intoxicating, panty-melting game of—

Focus, damn it.

"If you can't figure it out," I tell him, forcing myself back into the present, "then you're mine. I'm in charge."

"How many guesses do I get?" His devilish smile has deepened. He still looks at me now as he did back then, like there's no greater pleasure in all the world than engaging in these little competitions with me.

"As many as you like," I tell him. "But every time you guess wrong, you lose an article of clothing." I lace my fingers together, resisting the urge to reach out and yank him toward me. "If you run out of clothes to lose, then I win. If you use up all ten of your questions, you're allowed one final guess. If you still can't figure it out, then you've still lost, no matter how many clothes you might have. Otherwise this could go on all night." *And I'm not sure I'll make it that long.*

He considers this. "Do I get a bonus for guessing it before my ten questions are up?"

"You're very cocky tonight," I tease, my heart thudding against my ribs. "Already demanding additional prizes when you haven't even taken your first guess yet." *If he already knows what's going on, then why hasn't he said anything?* "Does this mean you agree to the rules?"

"Of course." He straightens in his seat, drawing my eyes back to those broad, perfect shoulders of his. "I never refuse a game."

"All right," I say lightly, leaning forward and taking the lid off of the dish between us. Our main course tonight is lamb with mint sauce, and my mouth waters as the rich aroma reaches my nose. *God, I'm starving. Forget the lamb—I could eat an entire horse tonight.* "Since you seem so sure of yourself, maybe you should make your first guess. I'm going to start eating."

Calder might be confident about his chances of winning this game, but he still takes a moment to think before speaking.

"These are our first holidays together as a married couple," he says finally. "And while it's been special to share it with my sister and Ward, it's important to make our own personal traditions."

I wait for him to go on as I serve myself some lamb, but when he doesn't, I glance up at him. "That's all?" True, this past summer we accepted the invitation from Louisa Cunningham and Ward Brannon to move into the Cunningham mansion with them, but while this rather untraditional living situation has some unique challenges, it hasn't exactly been difficult to find some time to ourselves in a house of this size.

Calder's nose wrinkles slightly. He really thought he'd figured it out. "Well, I thought—"

"I'm sorry, but you're wrong," I tell him. "And that means you need to lose an article of clothing."

His frown deepens slightly—but only for a second. Then the corner of his mouth tilts up again, and he shakes his head as he undoes his tie.

"I can see I'm in for a good challenge tonight," he says, pulling the tie from his neck and dropping it on the ground beside him. His eyes flash, and I feel like I'm staring down a wolf. *A sexy, sharp-eyed, silver-tongued wolf who knows exactly what effect he has on me.*

"Technically, I'd consider a tie an accessory and not an article of clothing," I say, trying to keep my voice even.

"Oh, no. We're not having that argument. Not tonight." Those nearly-black eyes study me across the table. "And I have a feeling I might need every last piece of what I'm wearing before this game is over."

"Only if you keep making silly guesses." I pull the lid off the second dish on the table. "Would you like some rosemary mashed potatoes?"

"A little food in my stomach might help," he says, reaching for the spoon. He serves me first— something for which I'm ridiculously grateful. I can't believe how ravenous I am tonight.

After we each have a plate, he grabs his glass and glances around. "Is there wine?"

"Oh, no. I must have forgotten it," I say with a shrug. "I guess we'll just have to make do without it." I smile. "That's one question down, by the way."

His brow wrinkles. "One ques—Lily, you know that wasn't one of my questions."

"I specified that you had ten yes or no questions. I never specified anything about the subject of those questions. By the rules you agreed to, you've officially used your first one."

He shakes his head again, but a throaty chuckle escapes his lips. "Yes, this will definitely be a challenge."

"You should know how these little games work by now," I say.

"I should," he admits. "And I guess this means I shouldn't take anything for granted." He cocks his head and studies me. "Here's my next question, then—does the occasion for this dinner specifically have to do with us? As a couple, I mean."

"Yes," I say, scooping up a bite of mashed potatoes. So far everything seems to be sitting well in my stomach, which is a relief. I never know these days.

He rubs his jaw. "It's not the anniversary of our engagement. Or our first kiss. Or the first time I had you." His eyelids drop slightly. "Though I wouldn't mind celebrating *that* particular anniversary every year."

My stomach flip-flops. I wouldn't mind celebrating that particular anniversary *right now*, but it isn't the reason for this special dinner.

He takes another bite of his food, apparently considering his next move. Finally he says, "I guess I'll have to use another question. Is this about an anniversary at all?"

"No," I say.

He nods, that hint of a smile still lingering on his lips. "Good. I would hate to think I'd forgotten something."

I match his grin. "It wouldn't be the first time a man has done so."

"But it would be the first for me." His eyes are sharp again, penetrating me in a way that makes me press my thighs together reflexively. "I haven't forgotten anything about our time together, Lily. I remember everything we've done. Every moment I've had you in my arms. And I'll never forget any detail of you or your body. Everything is burned in my mind forever—every curve, every freckle, every sensitive spot on your skin. Everything."

It's quite a claim, and though it leaves me breathless, I find myself wondering about the truth of his words. If he knows every part of me that well, shouldn't he have noticed *something* by now? Or maybe I haven't changed as much as I thought— maybe I only *feel* different.

"You've got seven questions left," I tell him. I'm suddenly very nervous, but I don't want to think about that. It's not like I can back out of this now. "Or would you prefer to take a guess?"

"Oh, no. I'm not making another guess. Not with your strict rules." His eyes glaze slightly as he sinks back into thought. "It pertains to us but isn't an anniversary," he says, brushing a thumb against his bottom lip. "Does it involve another member of our family?"

My pulse quickens. "In a way, I suppose it does. But it might help if you're more specific."

"Are those going to count as additional questions—" He tries to cut himself off, but it's too late. He's forfeited another question, and I raise my hand, spreading my fingers.

"Five questions left," I say. "And yes, every new question counts." We don't have much family between us, at least not yet. I'm going to make him work for this.

I can tell by the look he's giving me now that I'm going to pay for this later—but I'm not sure I'm entirely opposed to that punishment.

"All right," he says finally. "I see no other way around this than to play right into your hands. Does it involve Louisa?"

I shake my head and fold down a finger, counting his questions. "No."

"Ward?"

Another finger goes down. "Nope. And technically Ward and Lou aren't married yet, so he's not officially family."

His brow wrinkles. He's running out of ideas. "Your father?"

"Wrong again." One more finger down. "You have two questions left."

"And I'm beginning to think you've tricked me. I'm running out of family members very quickly." His eyes snap up to my face. "You are referring to a *living* member of our family, are you not?"

I suck my lip into my mouth, trying to decide how to answer this tricky question without giving it all away. After a moment, I say, "Well, I'm not talking about a dead member of this family, if that's what you're asking."

"Well, I've already named most of the living ones,"

he says, spreading his hands. "The only one left is little Ramona. It's not about her, is it?"

Ramona is our niece, the daughter of Lou and Ward, and she's only about seven months old. I can't believe Calder is this close to the truth and it still hasn't occurred to him yet. Can he really be this oblivious, especially after the last few weeks? Maybe *some* of the signs are only obvious to me, but it's hard to ignore the fact that I've had trouble keeping down some of my meals. I mean, I ended up getting sick all over the place on Christmas Eve. Did he just forget about that?

"It doesn't directly have to do with Ramona, no," I say finally. "But you're getting closer."

"But I'm out of questions," he says. "And if I recall correctly, that means I only have one guess." He's actually starting to look a little irritated with himself. He hates to lose—even when the punishment for a loss is hardly punishment at all.

And *I* am starting to feel a little irritated with him myself. *Seriously? How hasn't he figured it out yet?*

I lean back, waiting for the light bulb to go off in his brain. He has all the hints he needs. I'm not helping him anymore.

"I've been through every family member," he mutters to himself. "And how is Ramona the closest fit?"

I cross my arms. I can't believe the mention of little Ramona didn't give it away. Looks like I might win this one after all. I know we didn't exactly plan for this—not at this point in our lives, anyway—but is it really so far from his mind?

My irritation slips away, and in its place comes something far worse—fear. Fear that he's not ready.

That he'll be upset. That he'll think I was careless. Honestly, the idea that he might be anything but overjoyed at this news makes my stomach twist, and I suddenly feel like I'm going to be sick. I can't wait any longer.

"I told you this isn't about a deceased family member," I blurt. "But what if I also tell you this isn't about a current family member, either?"

The little furrow between his brows deepens. "Then I'd say you're pulling another one of your tricks, since that doesn't really leave anyone."

"Actually," I say, gripping the edge of the table to keep my hands from shaking, "it leaves *future* family members."

I can see the exact moment it finally—*finally*—hits him. His eyes go wide, and he becomes completely, perfectly still.

This is it. He's pissed. Upset. Disappointed.

He doesn't move. Doesn't say a word. After what seems like an eternity, his gaze slides down my body. Then back up again. To the empty wine glasses on the table. Back to my belly.

And still he doesn't say anything.

I can't take this. My stomach is so tight that I'm pretty sure I'm going to be sick all over this table. I leap to my feet, but before I can take a step, Calder is there, grabbing me by the arms.

"You're pregnant." His voice is softer than a whisper.

"Took you long enough to figure it out," I say. I'm shaking all over. "Don't look at me like that—"

Suddenly he crushes me against his chest, knocking the air right out of my lungs. And then before I can even suck in a breath, he pushes me back again. His gaze burns down into mine.

"You're sure?" he says.

His voice is still quiet, but his expression is so intense that it makes me a little dizzy.

"Well, I haven't been to the doctor yet," I manage. "But I've taken three pregnancy tests, and they all told me the same thing."

Something flickers across his face, and then he's yanking me against his chest again. Only this time his lips are coming down on my hair, my cheeks, my brow—anywhere he can reach.

I'm still trying to process this. "You... you're happy?"

"Happy?" His lips freeze on my hair. "Lily, I'm ecstatic. I'm..." He finishes that thought by grabbing my face and kissing me with a passion that leaves me seeing stars.

I cling to his shirt for dear life as my knees threaten to collapse. Just when I think I'm actually going to pass out in his arms, Calder pulls his face away from mine again and lets out a laugh.

"Lily, I... I can't believe... I just..." He laughs again. His whole face is alight. "This is just so..."

He looks practically *giddy*. I almost say so, but then he's kissing me again, chasing the breath right out of me, and I kiss him back with everything I have.

"I love you," he tells me between his kisses. "I love you so much."

Part of me would be content to stand here in his arms and kiss and laugh all night long, but I find myself pulling back, looking up into his bright, beaming face.

"Are you honestly telling me you had no idea?" I say. "Or were you just pulling my leg this entire time?"

He looks a little shamefaced. "It honestly didn't occur to me. The last time we discussed this we talked about waiting until we'd been married a couple of years, and I just thought—"

"I was taking my birth control, I promise," I tell him. "I don't know how this happened, but—"

"But I couldn't be happier." He leans forward until his forehead rests against mine. "I mean it, Lily. I… I can't even put into words how I feel right now. Even if this is a surprise."

A nervous laugh escapes my lips. "I still can't believe you didn't figure it out. What with the weird nausea I've been having—"

"Considering how much Louisa has been cooking for us recently, an upset stomach isn't *that* unusual."

I smile. "First of all, Lou is getting really good at cooking. She actually helped me make this meal for us. And didn't you find it slightly odd that I was the only one getting sick?"

His fingers spread against my lower back. "I thought it was a stomach bug, or—"

"And what about your claims that you know every inch of my body so well?" I tease. "You haven't noticed *anything* different about me these last few weeks?"

"Mm, well…" His hands slide slowly up my body. "I noticed that your breasts seemed a little more sensitive than usual, but I thought maybe I'd just become very, very good at stimulating them." His hands move over my breasts, one and then the other, and his thumbs slip between us to sweep across my nipples.

I try not to moan as the delicate nubs stiffen

against his touch.

"And you've been a little more tired than usual," he continues, "but I assumed I was just keeping you up too late night after night." He lowers his mouth and kisses me, his tongue slipping between my lips as his thumbs glide across my nipples again. I gasp against his mouth as pleasure sweeps through me.

The desire I've been suppressing all evening comes rushing forward like a tidal wave, and I grip Calder's shirt in my fists. He still has my breasts in his hands, and even the slightest movement of one of his fingers sends sensation shivering through them.

But before I can push him down on the table beside us, he pulls back. His face hovers just above mine, and though his eyes are glazed with desire, the brightness is still there, shining down on me like the sun.

"Lily, you've made me the happiest man in the world," he says. And then he laughs again.

God, I could listen to that sound all night.

His hands come up to cup my face, and his fingers sweep across my cheeks. "You're crying."

"I am?" I didn't even notice. But I'm so happy, so overwhelmed with emotion, that it's a marvel I'm even still standing.

"I love you," he tells me again. "The thought of having a baby with you, of watching our child grow inside of you... Lily, I can't imagine anything more extraordinary."

He doesn't wait for me to respond. Instead, he kisses me again, somehow even more eagerly than before, and I open myself to him, accepting all of his love and passion and tenderness. My tears are falling faster now, but I can't seem to stop them. I'm so happy that I feel like I would fall apart if it weren't for his arms around me.

"I love you," I manage to murmur against his lips.

"I love you," he says again. He pulls his lips away from mine and starts raining kisses on the rest of my face.

"You know," I say as his mouth starts a trail across my hair, "technically I'm in charge tonight."

His lips freeze against a spot just below my ear, and then he chuckles.

"I'm afraid, dear Lily, that you are mistaken," he says. "You said I was allowed one guess after my questions were up, and my guess was the correct one."

"Only because I spelled it out for you," I counter. "You'd already lost at that point, and I was tired of waiting for you to figure it out on your own."

"I would have guessed it."

"Then you did a very fine job of pretending you wouldn't. I think—" I squeal as he suddenly lifts me off my feet, throwing me over his shoulder. But almost as soon as he's done it, I feel his body stiffen beneath me.

"I shouldn't have done that," he says quickly, starting to set me down again. "I forgot—"

"Don't you start that with me," I say. "I swear, Calder, if you start treating me like I'm breakable just because I'm pregnant, we're going to have problems."

He laughs. "Pregnancy seems to be making you much bossier."

"I'm just getting started," I say. "And since I'm in charge tonight—"

This time I'm a little more prepared when he scoops me up, and if he's a little gentler when he throws me over his shoulder… well, I'll let it slide this time. Before long my belly will be too big for him to do this at all.

"We'll see who's in charge," he says, turning toward the door. "I think the only way to settle this is to go to bed this instant."

"I agree," I say. "Which is the only reason I'm not ordering you to put me down right now."

His arms tighten around me. "We'll see."

I try to kick him in the stomach, but he catches my leg before I can do any damage. But my fight is just for show. In my heart, I want nothing more than to sink into bed with him, to celebrate this news in his arms.

We've spent the last couple of years finding and building a family. And now, it's about to grow even bigger.

1

LILY

SEVEN MONTHS LATER
I'm going to kill Calder for doing this to me.

Sure, I knew pregnancy wouldn't exactly be a walk in the park. I always knew there'd be aches and pains and a number of physical surprises—but I wasn't prepared. Not at all.

It's like I'm a helpless child—I'm exhausted all the time and sometimes need help doing even the simplest tasks. God, I never thought I'd be looking forward to the day when I could tie my own shoes again. Did Lou have this much trouble when she was pregnant? Or am I just especially bad at this whole baby-growing thing?

My hand slides across the wide surface of my belly. It'll be worth it, I know. But I really wish I could speed up the whole pregnancy part and get to the having-a-baby-in-my-arms part. Or, you know, just be

16

able to go two hours without having to pee.

The baby shifts inside of me. I've taken to calling him Bubble—it felt weird referring to him as only "the baby," and Calder and I have been in hot debate over what we're actually going to name him—and he's grown into his temporary nickname quite well. He's an active little dude. And he's so big—every day my stomach seems impossibly bigger.

"You're energetic today," I tell him, pressing my fingers against the spot where his little foot keeps kicking.

Across the room, my sister-in-law lets out a laugh.

"He's as restless as you are," she says with a smile. "He knows it's almost time to be here."

"I still have a few weeks," I say. *God, that feels like a lifetime.*

I look over at Lou. We're in her room, getting ready for the afternoon's festivities, and she's surveying herself in the mirror. She's in a simple slip of white silk, and her blond hair hangs in loose waves around her shoulders.

On the surface, Calder and his sister seem completely different. He comes off as quite serious— sometimes positively *brooding*—while Lou seems more cheerful and effervescent. But once you get to know them, it's clear they're both Cunninghams through and through. They're both ruled by their passion— there's no "halfway" for a Cunningham, no mildness of emotion. They live and love with their full hearts.

Though they might look like night and day standing next to each other—Calder is tall with dark hair, while Lou is petite and blond, having dyed her hair for as long as I've known her—if you look closely, you can see the family resemblance. They both have the same dark eyes, and more than once I've been struck by how much their expressions resemble each other.

Lou and I have become much closer since Calder and I moved to the estate. Though technically Ward, Lou's husband-to-be, owns the property, I think it will always be the *Cunningham estate* to all of us. And it just feels right, the whole family living here together.

I glance down at little Ramona. She's currently playing on the stretch of carpet between me and Lou, babbling to herself as she pushes around some brightly colored blocks. She's growing more mobile every day—while she was a little late taking her first steps, she's starting to get the hang of it, and pretty soon she'll be running circles around all of us. I can't believe how quickly she's grown.

And soon you'll have one of your own, I think, shifting my gaze to Bubble. *If you can survive this pregnancy, at least.* Even now, my back is aching again, and I step over to an armchair and sink down onto the cushions.

"How did you manage it?" I ask Lou. I shift around against the pillows, but I can't seem to find a position that eases the pain in my lower back. My temples have started throbbing, too—it seems like every part of me hurts these days. *Now all I need is a leg cramp or two and I'll be a complete invalid.* Just last night I was woken by a charley horse that left me sobbing in pain—and left Calder nearly beside himself with worry.

Lou gives me a sympathetic look. "I managed it one day at a time. And I tried to remember what waited for me at the end of it all." She smiles down at her daughter.

You better be that cute, Bubble, I think at the little blob inside of me. He kicks in response.

Lou turns back toward the mirror. "Is my brother doing any better?"

"Honestly, I think he's having a harder time than I am," I admit. And *he* doesn't have to deal with his body doing all sorts of crazy things.

"That's typical, isn't it?" she says. "Ward was freaking out every step of the way with me. I swear, I stopped telling him about most of my aches and pains because he would just end up freaking out and making things worse."

I laugh. "I'm finding I have to use a similar strategy with Calder." Sometimes having an overprotective husband is kind of nice—but other times not so much. Calder has never been so attentive—or so nervous. Every time I'm experiencing the slightest bit of discomfort, I see the fear flicker in his eyes. He cares so much, loves me and this baby so badly, that he's terrified something will happen. He hates to let me out of his sight these days.

But I agree with Lou that his constant concern only ends up making me more anxious. I've stopped talking to him about the headaches and the backaches and the milder pains of pregnancy. Sometimes, though, it's impossible to hide my discomfort—like last night, when that leg cramp left me cursing and crying.

Just think of what's coming, I remind myself again. *You and Calder are going to have a baby. A son.* While Lou and Ward decided to wait until the birth to find out the gender of their child, neither Calder nor I had the patience for that. Now all we have to do is figure out a name. We've gone through dozens of baby name books, but we can't seem to decide on anything. Maybe I'll just end up calling him Bubble forever.

"What do you think, Ramona?" I ask the precious little girl at my feet. "Are you ready for your cousin Bubble to get here?"

Ramona looks up from her blocks at the sound of her name.

"Buh!" she cries, lifting a red block in her little fist. "Buh! Buh!"

"I think that's a *yes*," Lou says. She comes over and scoops her daughter up in her arms.

Ramona is a beautiful little baby. Her cheeks have grown rounder and rosier these last few months, and her reddish-gold curls are a thick halo around her head. Just looking at her warms my heart, and I find my hand tightening on my belly, tears filling my eyes as I think of the day very soon when I'll get to hold my own child in my arms. Calder's child.

Yes, all of the aches and pains will be worth it in the end.

"Ma," Ramona says, pressing her hand against Lou's cheek.

"Ma-*ma*," Lou corrects with a smile.

Ramona replies with a series of nonsense sounds and claps her hand against Lou's cheek a second time.

"She'll get it right eventually," Lou says. "She's already saying 'dada' all the time." She bounces her daughter on her hip. "Say 'mama,' sweetheart. Ma-*ma*."

"Ma," Ramona says again. "Buhhh!"

Lou laughs. "She's as stubborn as her dad."

"Here, let me take her," I say, rising and holding out my arms. "I'll hold her while you finish getting ready."

Lou passes her to me, and I settle Ramona on my

hip. It's a little awkward holding a fourteen-month-old with my belly the size that it is, but I'm happy—even *eager*—for the practice of dealing with a baby.

Ramona smiles at me and grabs a fistful of my hair. I can't believe how big she is already—it feels like only yesterday she was small enough to fit in the crook of my arm. So small she couldn't even lift her head on her own.

At the other end of the room, Lou has stepped into her dress. Now she twists awkwardly around, trying to reach the tiny zipper hidden beneath a strip of lace at the back.

"Here, let me help," I say, going over to her.

With Ramona in one arm, it's almost just as difficult for me to get the little zipper closed—but at least Lou didn't choose a gown with elaborate lacing or a hundred tiny pearl buttons or something. In spite of the fact that Lou grew up with ridiculous amounts of money, her style is relatively simple—and her wedding dress reflects just that. The bodice is covered with thin strips of delicate lace, and the plain chiffon skirt falls like water around her legs. The entire look is simple, pretty, and slightly bohemian—and it suits her perfectly.

"Have you decided what you want to do with your hair yet?" I ask her as I tuck the zipper away beneath the lace.

"I might need your help," she tells me, grabbing her phone and pulling up a picture. "I have some ribbon we can use." The photo she shows me features a messy bun of waves with a lacy ribbon woven through it—a style that will look gorgeous with the natural texture of Lou's hair.

"That will look beautiful on you," I tell her.

"Between the two of us, I think we can figure it out."

Lou and Ward decided to have their wedding here at the estate, just like Calder and I did, but their nuptials will be even simpler than ours—frankly, I'm pleased that they're having a wedding at all, since Lou wasn't sure she wanted much of a fuss. But her dark eyes are glowing as she surveys herself in the mirror, and I know she's glad they decided to have an actual ceremony. Sure, she and Ward are already living together and already have a child together—but there's something magical about making those marriage vows out loud, about taking that final, traditional step.

"How weird is this?" Lou says. "I was ready to pop with Ramona when you and Calder got married, and now you're pregnant at my wedding. We've traded places."

"I just wish I were a little more mobile," I say with a laugh. I've only been standing for a few minutes, and already my back has started to ache again. I should probably put Ramona down.

"That's the most frustrating part as you get down to the end," she says. She twists and brushes a finger through Ramona's curls. The little peanut is starting to get fussy, but she quiets a bit at her mother's touch.

"It's probably time for her nap, isn't it?" I say. "Or is she hungry? Do you want me to go pass her off to Ward?"

"We can just put her in the crib here. Ward offered to take her while I was getting ready, but I wanted her here with us. Sort of a special girls' afternoon before the big event." She scoops her daughter out of my arms and carries her over to the cradle in the corner of the room, humming softly to her.

I'm gathering together the tools I'll need to help Lou with her hair when my cell phone buzzes in my pocket. Calder ran out to grab a few last-minute things for the wedding, and I expect it to be him as I look at the screen. Instead, I find that it's a call coming in from the intercom at the estate's front gate.

"That's weird," I murmur. To Lou, I say, "What time is Martin coming?"

"About five." The Cunninghams' former private chef is working double duty tonight—in addition to bringing a special wedding dinner for us, he's going to be officiating the ceremony. But other than him, we aren't expecting any guests. Calder and I will be acting as both attendants and witnesses for Lou and Ward.

"There's someone at the gate," I tell her. I hit the button on my phone to stream the feed from the security camera we have pointed at the front gate. "It's a taxi. I can't see inside."

Lou has gone rigid. "Could it be a reporter?" Our family has had more than a few nightmarish run-ins with paparazzi and overeager reporters, and even though things have quieted down a little recently, I completely understand the anxiety I see on her face. We'll never truly escape them, and every time there's a big event in one of our lives, the fear comes back, hovering like a shadow beneath the joy and excitement.

But usually any reporters who trek all the way out here to the estate don't bother pressing the button on the gate—if they're determined enough to make it this far, they usually try to sneak their way onto the property. They know we won't willingly let them in.

"Let me see," I say. I hit a button and raise the cell to my ear. "This is Lily Cunningham," I say, knowing our mysterious visitor will hear me through the intercom on the call box. "Who is this?"

There's a crackle in my ear as our guest hits the button on the call box. Now that my phone is at my ear, I can't see the person as he or she leans out of the car window, but the voice that comes through is crystal clear.

"Lily, honey," comes a vaguely familiar female voice. "Is that really you?"

My blood goes cold. The phone nearly falls out of my hand.

"What is it?" Lou says, apparently alarmed by the look on my face. "Who's here?"

"I…" Without thinking about it, I find myself hitting the button to open the gate. I need to see her. I need to confirm this with my own eyes. To Lou I say, "I'll go take care of it. You go find that ribbon for your hair. I'll be right back."

I hurry out the door and down the steps, my mind racing. Bubble starts squirming inside of me, and I rub my belly.

"Don't worry," I tell him. "It's just a little complication, that's all. Your mama is going to take care of this." But inside, my mind is spinning. Maybe I misheard that voice. Maybe all the pregnancy hormones have screwed up my brain and I'm hearing things. Because it can't be *her*. It just can't.

God, I wish Calder were here right now.

When I reach the front door, the taxi has already parked out front. I stay at the top of the steps, frozen in place.

It can't be her. There's no way.

And honestly, I hardly recognize the woman who steps out of the back of the cab. Her shoulder-length hair has been dyed a burgundy shade of red, a hue that nearly matches the color on her lips. Her clothes are just as bright—far brighter than anything I can remember her wearing—and between her royal blue pencil skirt and ruffled, pattern shirt she reminds me of some sort of exotic bird.

No, this isn't her. She looks nothing like I remember.

But then she turns toward me, and the sun catches her face just so—and in that instant, the rush of recognition hits me like a punch to the gut. In that moment, I see her—beneath the colors and the makeup, I find the soft, loving face of that woman I knew so many years ago. The woman I never thought I'd see ever again.

My mom.

No, no… it can't be…

But now she's seen me. She freezes when her eyes meet mine, and then her lips spread into a wide smile.

"Honey!" she exclaims. "Look at you!"

I'm speechless. Rooted at the top of the steps. She comes toward me, beaming and waving as if she's only been gone for a couple of days. In reality, it's been more like twenty years.

Twenty years. Two decades since this woman walked out of my life and abandoned me and my dad. This has to be a dream. A hallucination. God, why isn't Calder here?

She practically bounds up the steps, and I can see her eyes taking everything in—the elaborate grounds around us, the huge house behind me, and finally, *me*. And she never stops smiling through that red lipstick.

"Look at you," she says again when she reaches me. "Look how big you are! Oh, honey, I didn't realize you were so far along already."

I don't know what to do. What to say. Finally, I find my voice. "What are you doing here?" Once that question escapes my lips, the rest come quickly behind: "How did you know where I was? Why have you come? And how did you know I was pregnant?" A sudden thought occurs to me. "Did Dad tell you? Have you been talking to Dad?" That doesn't make any sense—Dad would never keep something like that from me.

But this woman in front of me doesn't seem the least bit fazed by my barrage of questions.

"Oh, honey, don't be silly," she says. "*Everyone* knows that you're pregnant. And that you're living here on the Cunningham property. Have you forgotten that you're a tabloid star?" She gives a wave of her hand. "But that's all old news. All the magazines have moved on to the latest drama with the Fontaines or with that weird musician with the shark tattoo—what's his name again?"

I shake my head, still trying to process this. "You have to leave."

She blinks. "But I've only just arrived."

"I don't care. You have to go." I can't deal with this, not right now. Pain has started to pulse in my temples again. I'm experiencing too many emotions right now—shock, confusion, fear, anger—and I'm not prepared to deal with any of them. Not on top of everything else.

"Sweetheart," she says again, more quietly this time. "I know this must be a surprise, but—"

"A surprise?" I say, incredulous. "This is a little bit more than a surprise." *This is a nightmare. I can't deal with this right now.* "I don't understand why you're here."

26

She tilts her head slightly, and once again, I see a glimpse of the woman I once knew—the woman who I thought would continue to exist solely in my memories.

"I'm here to see you, of course," she says softly. Tentatively, she reaches out and brushes her fingers against my cheek—but I flinch beneath her touch. "It's been a long time, Lily."

So long that this woman is practically a stranger. In spite of myself, I find myself looking closer at her, trying to find more of the pieces I recognize. It's hard. Her hair is shorter than it used to be—and red, as I noticed before, when I remember her natural shade as being closer to a dirty blond. Up close I can see the silver at the roots—and the wrinkles beneath her makeup. That's what hits me the hardest—seeing how old she looks. She's a couple of decades past the thirty-something woman who lives in my head. Seeing her like this is a stark reminder of how much time has passed. How much life I've lived without her.

"It's been too long, honey," she says. "And you've become such a beautiful woman since the last time I saw you." Her eyes glisten, almost as if she's fighting back tears.

But I jerk away. "The only reason it's been so long is because you decided to walk out on me and Dad."

Her smile slips. "Oh, sweetheart, I know I can't expect you to understand, but—"

"You're right—I don't understand." *This can't be happening right now.* "It's been twenty years. Twenty *years*, and you haven't tried to call me or write me a letter or anything. You just disappeared from my life. From Dad's life." I reach out for the railing, still in shock. Part of me still refuses to believe that she's actually here, that this isn't some sort of trick. I need Calder. I need someone here to tell me that this isn't a cruel joke.

I can't read the expression on my mom's face.

"I had my reasons for leaving, Lily," she says.

Maybe she did, and maybe she didn't. But I feel like I'm drowning. "And I have my reasons for asking you to leave."

"Lily, I just—"

"Get off this property," I whisper. "Now." I force myself to take a step back toward the door, but I can't bring myself to tear my eyes away from her.

"Lily, please," she says, her voice just as soft as mine. "I just want to make things right."

Numbness has set in, my shock overtaking all of my other emotions. But I find my voice. "You've had twenty years to make things right."

"And you know what they say—it's better late than never." She lets out a sigh. "Oh, honey, you have no idea how sorry I am. If I could go back, I'd—well, let's just say I'd do things differently. But I can't take back those choices now. I made them, and for better or for worse, I have to live with them. But sweetheart, I can choose to make things right now. Here in the present."

"It's not that simple," I say through the numbness.

"Just let me try," she pleads. "Lily, sweetheart, I'm so sorry. I know nothing I say or do can make it up to you, but I'm not asking for your forgiveness. Or even your understanding. I'm just asking to talk."

My heart is beating too quickly. Bubble is moving around inside of me, probably sensing my distress.

"I'm happy," I say. My voice is soft, but I know she can hear me. "I've lived a good life so far, even though you weren't there. Maybe *because* you weren't there. I've found my way. Found joy even though you weren't there to support me." I swallow. "Give me one good reason why I should talk to you."

She tilts her head, and she looks so sad that for a split second, through the shocked numbness, I feel like my own heart is breaking—but why? This woman abandoned me and my dad. I shouldn't be feeling anything for her. She doesn't deserve it.

"You're having a baby, honey," she says, taking a tentative step toward me. "If a girl needs her mother at any point in her life, it's then."

I shake my head again. "I'm already surrounded by people who love and support me. I don't need you anymore." I take another step back toward the door.

"There's nothing quite like it, being a mother," she says, more to herself than to me. "It's the most wonderful thing in the world... and at the same time, it's also the most difficult."

There's a lump in my throat, but I force myself to take another step.

"You were quite the stubborn little baby," she continues, and a hint of a smile passes across her lips. "You didn't cry very much, but when you did, you could have woken the dead. You always knew exactly how to get what you wanted."

I don't want to hear this. Don't want to notice the tenderness I now see in her face. Don't want to hear the affection in her voice. It took me *years* to come to terms with the fact that she was gone and she wasn't coming back. To acknowledge that she might actually have loved me in some way feels like I'm betraying the little girl who experienced that pain. But her words sink into my heart, and I feel my eyes start to ache.

It's just the pregnancy, I tell myself. *You have no control over your emotions anymore. Just take a deep breath and ask your mom again to leave.* If Calder were here, he'd tell her off in an instant.

But when I try to find the words, my tongue feels too thick and dry.

"Sweetheart," my mother says, holding out her arms to me. There are tears in her eyes, too—there's no denying that now. And I swear I hear the desperation in her voice, the years of emotions she's kept bottled up inside.

I don't want to move, but I do. My feet stumble forward, and before I know it, my arms are around her. And hers are around me—or as close as they can be, given the Bubble wedged between us.

She smells the same—God, how is that even possible? I didn't even think I remembered the way she smelled, but apparently I do. She feels so familiar. So comfortable.

"Mom," I manage to choke out as the tears start to fall.

She sniffles and tightens her hold on me. "Oh, honey."

In my belly, Bubble begins to squirm and kick. He always seems to get more active when I'm emotional, and even though I don't know exactly what I'm feeling, my emotions are off the charts right now. And Bubble insists on having his say. He gives an especially energetic kick, and it's powerful enough that my mom feels it, too. She jumps in surprise, then lets out a laugh.

"Quite the little athlete you've got in there," she says, pulling back and wiping a tear off her cheek.

"Yes, he hardly sits still anymore," I say, giving my own face a quick sweep with my sleeve. "My doctor says he's quite strong."

Her eyes gleam. "It's a boy?"

I nod.

"Oh, that's wonderful," she says, placing her hand on my belly. "Have you picked out a name yet?"

It's strange to have her touch me so intimately—after so many years, there's something very foreign about it. And my emotions are still too complicated.

"Calder and I haven't decided on anything yet," I say. "But we'll figure it out before the time comes."

She's still rubbing my belly, and I'm not sure what to do. Part of me wants to cringe away from that familiar touch—my feelings are much too raw for this—but she's still my mom, after all. And this is still her grandchild. *This can't really be happening…*

She seems to be following a similar line of thought. "My first grandbaby. He's going to be a looker, that's for sure." Her eyes rise once more to the house behind me. "Is your husband around? I want to meet him."

I give a nervous laugh and step back, smoothing my hand down my dress, suddenly remembering what's on the schedule for today. "Calder's out running errands. Look, I…" *What's the best way to handle this?* "I know we have a lot to catch up on, but I'm not sure today is the best day for this."

Her eyes widen slightly and her smile falls, and I suppose I can't blame her for being surprised or even offended—after all, our reunion is a pretty big deal to both of us—but on the other hand, she *did* show up without any warning. And it's not exactly my place to invite her to Lou and Ward's private wedding

31

ceremony.

"Can we meet somewhere tomorrow?" I ask her. "Do lunch or something? Where are you staying?"

She gives a little shrug and puts her smile back on. "Oh, I haven't figured that out yet, sweetheart. I was too excited to see you."

Something about her answer doesn't sit right with me. I'm still a little confused about why she showed up *now*, on today of all days, when she claims she's known about my marriage and pregnancy for some time. And her flippancy only adds to the unsteady feeling in my stomach.

"Why are you here, Mom?" I ask. "If you wanted to see me, why did you wait so long? Why now?"

"It's a complicated story," my mom says, straightening. She flicks some of her russet-colored hair over her shoulder.

"That doesn't mean I don't need to hear it." I search her face, but she doesn't give anything away.

"Can't a mother just want to see her daughter?" she asks with a tentative smile.

Part of me wants to believe that's all it is—but I don't have time to press any further right now. I have to help Lou with her hair—and get myself ready for the wedding as well.

"We can talk about this some more tomorrow," I say. I glance behind her toward the taxi, which is still waiting. "Why don't you take your cab into town and find a hotel? We can meet for lunch or something." *And that will give me time to process all of this. And talk to Calder.*

I start to back toward the door again, but my mom throws up an arm.

"Lily, wait. I…" There's a slight tremble in her

32

voice that wasn't there before. "I have nowhere else to go."

My fingers freeze on the doorknob. "What do you mean? There are plenty of hotels in Barberville, I promise."

"It's not that," she says. "I just… I had to leave, Lily. There—well, there was a man. I've been living with him these past six years, and… Oh, honey, he wasn't the man I thought he was. He took everything I have in the world. All of my money. And when I realized what he was doing I had to get out of there, and it took most of the cash I had left just to get here." Her heels shift on the stone. "I ended up here without even really trying. I don't know why—I mean, of course I wanted to see you, sweetheart, but I'd been afraid for so long of… of facing you after what I did. But something told me to come here. And when I saw you just now I… I couldn't believe I'd waited so long to do this. But oh, honey, I don't know what to do now."

Neither do I.

Damn it, Lily. Just be strong and tell her to go. You don't owe her anything. She's only been here for five minutes and you're already an emotional mess. You can't deal with this drama right now. You have a baby to think about. But the other voice in my head is just as strong: *But she's your mom. A part of you has always missed her, even when you told yourself you were strong enough to get on without her. That part of you will always need her, just a little bit. And it sounds like she needs your help right now.*

It's obvious that she's still not telling me everything. She only showed up here because she's desperate—not because she had a sudden crisis of conscience. But she's still my mom. She'll always be my mom. And I'll never forgive myself if I don't help her.

"Fine," I hear myself saying, as if from far away. "You can come in. I'll find you a place to stay for a couple of days until you figure out your next step." I start to open the door. "But this doesn't mean that everything is good between us."

She dabs her eyes. "Oh, honey—"

"And stop calling me that," I say. I might have succumbed to my feelings for a minute there, but the numbness is setting in again. "I'm not your 'honey.' Or your 'sweetheart.' Or anything else. As far as I'm concerned, I'm hardly even your daughter."

She doesn't say anything for a long moment. But then she lifts her chin. "You'll always be my 'honey,' no matter what. In my heart, no matter where I was, you were always still my baby. And you always will be."

I turn away, refusing to acknowledge her with even a look. "Do you have any bags?"

"Just one. I'll go get it from the taxi. Oh, Lily, darling, thank you so much."

Her heels clatter back down the steps to the cab, but I stay where I am. This is insane, but I'm not sure what other choice I have. I'll put her in one of the guest rooms during the wedding. And I should give Dad a call tonight—I don't want her surprising him like she surprised me, especially since Dad is going to be remarried soon.

Bubble gives my insides another vigorous kick.

"I know," I say to him, rubbing the spot. "But we'll get through this. If anything, she'll remind me of all the things I *shouldn't* do when you finally arrive."

He gives another kick as if in agreement.

Yes, we'll figure this out. But one thing's for certain—the final leg of my pregnancy is about to get even more difficult.

2
WARD

I thought I was ready for this—but fuck me, I was wrong.

I want to punch something. Just to release some of this energy. Just to *do something*. Because standing here waiting around for the ceremony to start isn't working. It's almost funny—I mean, I've wanted this forever. I tried to convince Lou to marry me from the moment I found out she was pregnant. I'm not supposed to be nervous now. And I'm pretty sure I'm not supposed to find myself aching for a fight right before I marry the woman I love.

Is Lou this anxious? Is she fidgety and distracted? Is she wondering why she ever agreed to marry a crazy oaf like me?

I've never wanted anything more than this in my entire life—so why am I so damn jumpy?

I jerk a hand through my hair. I want to fix something. Grab my toolkit and get hammering on one of my projects. Or grab a sledgehammer and tear through some old drywall. Smash something. But I'm already dressed. Already here. And anyway I'm pretty sure Lou wouldn't appreciate it if I got dust and debris all over my wedding clothes.

Who am I kidding? If there's anyone who wouldn't care about something like that, it's Lou. She told me I shouldn't wear a tux—said it wouldn't look like me. But I'll be damned if I don't look good for her today. I might not be in a tux, but I'm in my nicest pair of slacks and a button-down shirt I bought especially for the occasion. Dark blue—what she says is her favorite color on me. I'm even wearing a tie.

I tug at the tie. I feel like I've forgotten something. What else am I supposed to do? How am I supposed to prepare for this? This is the most important day in my life—or second most important, at least. Even our wedding day might not top the day Lou gave birth to our daughter. Ramona and Lou are the brightest parts of my life—and now that Lou and I are getting married, they'll be protected in case anything ever happens to me. That is worth everything.

So why do I feel like I'm about to hurl?

I slide my hand into my pocket. The folded sheet of paper with my vows is still safely in there. I guess as long as I have that, I'm good, right?

Maybe I should have asked Calder about how to handle this. My future brother-in-law and I are almost friends these days—at least as much as we can be, considering I knocked up his sister and inherited his family's estate from my billionaire asshat of a father. But it's too late for that now. Lou should be here any minute.

I shift my weight and look up. All around me, the

37

walls of the hedge maze rise toward the sky. This maze is where Lou and I fell in love. Where I proposed. And today, it'll be the place where we promise ourselves to each other forever. We decided to have our ceremony in the courtyard right at the heart of the labyrinth.

Martin is watching me. I'd almost forgotten the old guy was here, that's how anxious I am. But he reaches out and puts his hand on my shoulder. "It's normal to be nervous."

I straighten my tie. "I know."

His smile deepens. "Louisa couldn't have done better."

In spite of my nerves, I find myself smiling, too. "Actually, I'm the one who couldn't do better." Lou is everything to me. She's the most beautiful, most amazing woman I've ever met. I love everything about her—her energy, her passion, her spontaneity, her heart. And I love all the crazy parts of her, too. I've never known anyone else like her in my entire life, and after going through hell and back together, I can't imagine spending the rest of my life with anyone else. I pray every day that I can be the man she deserves—especially now that we have a daughter together.

Suddenly, Martin lifts his hand from my shoulder. "It's time."

I straighten my shoulders. *This is it*. Whether I think I'm ready or not, I'm about to get married.

I look across the courtyard, toward the opening in the hedges. There's no music, but there doesn't need to be. The only thing that matters is her. My Lou.

Lily comes first with Ramona in her arms. My little girl is being her normal, energetic self, and she squirms and squeals when she sees me, reaching out one chubby little hand in my direction. I wave to her but otherwise hold my place. Part of me longs to take my daughter from Lily, to have her in my arms while I watch Lou walk down the aisle, but I'm not sure I trust myself to hold anything important right now. Still, I don't take my eyes off of Ramona as Lily comes closer. My daughter looks more like Lou every day. I already see her mother's spirit in her eyes. She's going to be a troublemaker, this one. And every bit as vibrant and adventurous as Lou.

Lily has reached us now, and she smiles at me before going to stand on the opposite side of Martin. Ramona wiggles in her arms, still reaching for me.

"Da! Da da da!" she squeals.

I grin, and Martin stifles a chuckle as Lily bounces my daughter on her hip, trying to calm her.

It's then that I hear the rustle of footsteps behind us, and I turn back toward the entrance to the courtyard.

And my heart stops.

Holy shit. Lou looks... radiant. Breathtaking. Like an angel come to life. I've always thought she was beautiful, but fuck me, this is... something else.

She shines. I can't take my eyes off of her. I don't know a damn thing about wedding dresses or hairstyles or any of that crap, but I know what I'm seeing right now. I know what I'm feeling as I look at her dressed like this. The whole thing is just... It's just...

My eyes lock on hers, and in the depths of her gaze I see the bright spark that has pulled me under her spell again and again. She's never looked so beautiful in all her life.

Her brother is walking her down the aisle, but I don't see anyone but her. With every step she takes toward me, her smile gets bigger. Her eyes brighter.

And it's taking every ounce of my willpower not to run forward and take her in my arms and kiss her breathless.

It takes a damn eternity for her to reach me—an eternity of beauty and pleasure and pure joy. And then Calder is holding her hand out to me, and I take her fingers in mine and grip them way too hard.

"Take care of her," Calder murmurs. I tear my eyes away from Lou just long enough to see the serious look in her brother's eyes—but there's something else there, too. He'll be watching me, I know—I can't imagine he'll ever stop feeling protective of his little sister—but I can also see the respect there, the trust. He trusts me to take care of Lou. And I will. I'll love her and cherish her for every moment of the rest of my life.

And then Calder is stepping aside, and it's just me and Lou again. I'm grinning so hard my cheeks have started to ache. Lou's eyes are still locked on mine, shining right through me, and my throat starts to burn. *Pull it together, man.*

Martin starts talking, but there's still nothing else in the world to me but Lou—and Ramona, who's still squirming in Lily's arms just behind my bride. Our little daughter gurgles and squeals, and between her tiny nonsense noises she starts repeating her latest words.

"Da!" she says. "Da da! Nuhhhhn! Da!"

Lou lets out a soft laugh, which only seems to encourage Ramona.

"Maaa!" Ramona cries. "Naaa! Ma! Da!

Nuuuhnnn!"

Lily makes some soothing sounds to her and bounces her gently in her arms. But Ramona is having none of it.

"Nuuuuuuuhnnnn!" she says, her little voice getting stronger. "Maaaaaa!"

I know that sound. She's getting ready to scream. As far as these things go, Ramona's been a pretty easy, happy baby—but when she gets worked up, I swear that kid is louder than an air horn. And from the way her face is scrunching up right now, I know we're in for a full tantrum.

Lou knows it, too. I can see it in her eyes. She stifles another laugh and squeezes my fingers, but we both know that in a few seconds we won't be able to ignore her.

Even Martin has started chuckling as he tries to deliver his lines. Finally Lou releases my hands and twists around toward Lily.

"Here," she says with a laugh. "I better take her." And she does, lifting our daughter into her arms and turning back to face me.

Ramona is still squirming and babbling—but she seems to have gotten what she wanted. She no longer looks like she's about to scream. Lou rocks her gently with one arm and nods to Martin that he should continue before reaching toward me with her free hand. I take her fingers in mine again.

Seeing Lou in her wedding gown with our daughter nestled against her somehow makes her even more beautiful. One of her curls has come loose, and it sways against her neck as she rocks Ramona. Our daughter has started to calm a little more, but she still coos and babbles to us. Martin begins speaking again, but his words continue to go in one ear and out the other as I stare at the two most important people in my life. My girls.

"And now," Martin says, "for the exchanging of vows."

That's my cue. With my free hand—I'll be damned if I let go of Lou—I reach into my pocket and pull out the sheet of paper I've been keeping there. But my eyes can't seem to focus on the words.

"Lou," I say, looking back up at her. "I don't know what to say."

She gives me an encouraging smile, and Ramona waves her little fist at me and says "Dada!"

"I love you," I tell her. "More than anything. You and Ramona both. And I want to spend the rest of my life protecting you, supporting you, and loving you with all my heart. You are my life. My light. I've never met anyone with your spirit, your energy, your strength. You've made me happier than I ever expected I could be. And you've given me a beautiful daughter."

Her hand tightens on mine, and there's a telltale wet glimmer in her eyes.

"I will go anywhere with you," I continue. "Take on anything. Protect you in every way that I can. And if there's ever anything I can't defeat for you, I'll hold your hand and face it with you. I will never leave your side." I swallow down the lump in my throat. "I've wanted this for a long time, Lou. To officially be a family. You've made me the happiest man in the world, and I promise that no matter what happens, I will spend the rest of my life repaying you for what you've given me."

She blinks back tears, but her smile is still wide and

bright. And Ramona seems just as pleased, even if she can't understand what I just said. She gives a happy little cry and reaches toward me.

"Would you like to hold her?" Lou asks softly.

I nod. I still feel... well, not quite like myself, but I've found my footing and I trust myself not to drop Ramona now. Lou passes our daughter into my arms and flicks a tear away before straightening again.

"You found me when I was lost," she says. "When no one else could. You saw parts of me that I had yet to see. You brought me back from the darkness." She blinks again, and her tears catch in her lashes and shine like diamonds. "You've been so good to me. Better than I thought I deserved. And you've given me more than I could ever ask for—including our daughter, the most precious gift of all. I love you with my whole heart, and I will continue to do so, no matter what happens, until the day that I die. I still can't believe the universe decided to send you to me. That I get to spend my life with the most amazing guy who ever lived." A tinkling laugh escapes her lips as she wipes her eyes, and my smile widens.

In my arms, Ramona yells, "Maaa!" Lou laughs again.

"This is perfect," she continues. "I never thought I could be this happy. But I am, because of you. And I promise I'll try to make every day of the rest of our lives just as happy for you. I promise to find you if you ever get lost. I promise to trust you with my deepest fears and protect you from yours in return. And I promise to never ever give you anything less than my whole heart."

Ramona has discovered the buttons on the front of my shirt, and she tries to grab one with her chubby fingers, releasing a gurgling laugh when she can't quite do it. Which makes Lou laugh once more, and me too—and Martin and Lily and Calder, until we're all laughing and crying and Lou is leaning forward and kissing me, even though I'm pretty sure we haven't gotten to that part of the ceremony yet.

I kiss her in return. I want to pull her closer, press her body snugly against mine and feel every bit of her against me, but that's impossible with Ramona in my arms. Still, I can't think of a more perfect first moment of our married life—Lou's soft, warm lips against mine, her hands gripping my shirt, and our daughter, the perfect creation of our love, held between us. I'm pretty sure I have the most beautiful family that ever existed.

And I'd do anything to protect them.

"Uh, I believe we've forgotten to exchange the rings," Martin says with a grin when Lou and I finally come up for air.

So we do—a bit awkwardly, since Ramona keeps trying to grab the rings out of our hands as we slide them onto each other's fingers.

"I now pronounce you husband and wife," Martin says.

Well, I'm not going to pass up a chance to kiss Lou again. With my free hand, I pull her toward me once more, and she grabs my neck and yanks my mouth down to hers.

God, I love this girl.

When we come apart again, Lily and Calder both step forward. Lily has tears running down her cheeks, and she pulls Lou into a hug. Calder claps me firmly on the shoulder. I'd shake his hand—and Martin's, too—but Ramona's in my right arm, so I have to settle for giving each of them a nod and a "Thank you," through my smile.

Ramona is writhing and waving her arms, demanding to be the center of attention once again. I shift her to my side, and she giggles and cries, "Dada! Ga ga ga!" as I reach for Lou.

Lou's hand is waiting for mine. Our fingers interlace, her smaller, softer ones nearly disappearing in my grip. She's still grinning at me, her whole face shining, and once again I see her as an angel, so beautiful and full of light that she can't possibly be real.

We walk back through the maze together, hand in hand. The others probably follow, but I don't look back to see. Right now, the only people who matter are the woman at my side and the child in my arms.

We're married. Lou is my *wife*. God, I almost can't believe it. The nerves haven't left—not even close—but now that anxious energy is joined by a happiness so intense that I don't know what to do with myself. I want to shout, run, fight… and kiss Lou until she can't breathe.

These two girls are my duty now. From the beginning, I would have given anything—even my life—for either of them, but now that we've made this official, I feel the pressure, the promise, even more deeply.

"We're married." Lou's voice is so soft that I almost don't hear it at all. When I look down at her, I see the same wonder in her eyes that I feel deep in my chest—and I know that I'm not the only one feeling a little overwhelmed right now.

"It's official," I say lightly, squeezing her fingers. "I'm not letting you go now."

"And I'm not letting you go, either," she says, squeezing my hand right back. Her smile widens. "Who'd have guessed on that first day we met that we'd end up here?"

Oh, I remember that day well. I was a handyman here at the estate—only it was called Huntington Manor then, and in the process of becoming a luxury resort under the ownership of Edward Carolson, my father—and I'd been going about my business, just doing my job, when Lou walked by me. I wanted her from the moment I saw her. And when she found me shortly afterward, when she came up to me and grabbed me and kissed me without even knowing my name… well, it's enough to break a man. It's the sort of thing that burns its way into your blood and never leaves. And everything that has come after, every moment I've spent with Lou since, has only deepened that feeling.

It's crazy to think we've made it here.

Lou and I don't release each other's hands until we reach the formal dining room. Normally we eat our meals in a smaller room next to the kitchen, but I'll be damned if we don't use the nicest room in the house for our wedding dinner. Martin's sous chef has been in the kitchen prepping for the last couple of hours, and when I glance behind us I realize that Martin has apparently slipped away to join him. Only Lily and Calder are here with us, but Lily pauses at the door.

"I'll be right back," she says. "Can I grab you guys anything?"

It's Lou who speaks. "Oh! We've forgotten the champagne we set aside for tonight."

"I can grab that," Calder says. "I also took the liberty of getting you two a couple of special bottles of wine to celebrate—one for tonight, and another to open on one of your future anniversaries."

And just like that, Lou and I are alone again.

"Lily's mother is here," Lou says quietly to me.

"What?" That's news to me—I didn't know we were expecting anyone but Martin and his sous chef here today. I frown, trying to remember what I know about Lily's mom—which isn't much. "I didn't realize her mom was around. I've only ever heard her talk about her dad."

Lou shrugs. "She showed up out of the blue. Apparently told Lily she needed help and had nowhere else to go." She leans over and pushes a reddish curl out of Ramona's eyes. "She left when Lily was pretty young—about seven, I think."

Wait—so this woman abandoned her seven-year-old daughter? Anger shoots through me, and my whole body tenses—until I remember that I still have *my* daughter in my arms. I force my body to relax and look down at Ramona. All the excitement of the day has finally worn her out, and her eyelids droop as she tries to fight sleep. I glance back up at Lou, and I can tell from the look in her eyes that there's more to this than she's saying. "Should we be worried about anything?"

Lou shrugs again, and the movement makes that loose curl against her neck sway gently. "I don't know. Lily is—well, Lily's got a lot on her plate right now, you know? I'm worried about her. The pregnancy's been so difficult for her, and it must be hard to see her mom after all this time, no matter why she's here. But I can also see why she'd want to have her around." She bites her lip. "She promised her mom wouldn't get in the way, that we wouldn't even know she was here."

"Well, there's no reason she has to hide her," I say. "This is Lily's home, too. She's welcome to have any guests she likes, whenever she likes. And family is always welcome." I frown. "Should we invite her down to dinner? There's no reason the woman has to hunker down in her room like a criminal." *Even if she did abandon her child—one of the most unforgivable sins I can think of.* Considering I was a grown adult before I even met my father, I know exactly what that can do to a kid.

But Lou shakes her head. "I asked Lily the same thing, and I think she'd prefer to hold off introductions for a day or two—at least until she figures out what's going on and how she feels about everything."

"That's fair," I say. And honestly, I'm not sure how I feel about having that woman sit in on our wedding dinner. Still, Lily's officially family now—and as untraditional as our arrangement here is, that means something. Her family is my family, too. And Lily gets to make the call about whether she wants this woman in our lives. All of us in this house have known too much loss, spent so much of our adult lives looking for that elusive *family*, that I'm not about to push away anyone God or the universe decides to throw our way.

My eyes fall back to our daughter. I can't imagine leaving her, not for any reason in the entire world. What kind of monster can look at their own kid, their flesh and blood, and then walk away from that?

Lou's hand brushes gently against my cheek, and I realize I'm clenching my jaw.

"Lily will figure it out," she whispers. "Tonight,

you and I have more important things to think about."

If there's anything that can melt away the bitterness and resentment that have filled me, it's Lou's smile. Or that mischievous look in her deep brown eyes that promises both love and pleasure—tonight and beyond.

That's right. It's your wedding day, you fucking idiot. And we're just getting started. I'm not going to let anything spoil my wedding dinner with Lou—or our wedding night.

"Why don't you go put Ramona in her highchair?" Lou says, gesturing toward the table. "We haven't had a proper married kiss yet."

I'm only too happy to oblige. Ramona is much more subdued now, and I carefully place her into her highchair. The moment I've buckled her in, Lou is tugging me around toward her.

When her lips meet mine, I lose all control. All of the tension and emotion of the day seems to explode through me at once, and she gasps beneath the force of my kiss. I love her. I need her. My *wife*.

I twist her and push her back toward the wall. I've spent the last hour admiring how ethereally beautiful she looks today, and she's finally—*finally*—mine to do with as I please.

She seems just as eager. Her fingers dig into my back. Her lips and teeth and tongue fight desperately with mine, matching my hunger. We've kissed a thousand times before. It shouldn't be any different now that we're married. But it is. Before, we were joined in every way except one—now, that final barrier has been crossed. There's nothing between us anymore.

I want to drink every breath from her. Pull down her hair and twist my fingers through those beautiful, tempting curls. Slide up her dress and take her while she's still wrapped in that pure white fabric.

My fingers are pulling on her skirt when a throat clears behind us.

It's all I can do to tear my face away from Lou's. But oh yeah—we're expecting company for dinner. When I look back over my shoulder, my new brother-in-law is standing in the doorway, looking a little pissed at finding us like this.

I know I should feel bad—but I don't, not even a little bit. In fact, I'm pretty sure I've got a shit-eating grin on my face right now, in spite of the fact that Calder is giving me the stink eye.

"Don't look at him like that, Calder," Lou says, not the least bit embarrassed. "We're married now. You don't have to get all angry and protective anymore."

Calder's frown only deepens. "Forgive me if I'm not particularly pleased to see my sister pushed up against a wall like—"

"It's not like I've never walked in on you and Lily before," she returns, laughing now. "And I hate to break it to you, Calder, but Ward and I have sex. And we—"

"Let's just leave it at that," I say. I'd rather not get murdered by my wife's brother on our wedding night.

I straighten Lou's dress—and give her one more kiss on the cheek—before leading us back over to the table. I have a feeling that Calder would rather pretend his younger sister is completely innocent—but I guess I would too, if I had a little sister. So I can't really blame the guy.

I'll take it easy on him, I tell myself. *There's no reason to be sticking my tongue down his sister's throat right in front of him.* Still, one glance over at Lou—whose flushed cheeks and swollen lips are giving my cock all sorts of dangerous ideas—and I feel the need burn through me. When no one's looking, I quickly readjust my pants. I need to control myself. Ignore all of my baser impulses until later tonight.

It seems like a totally doable goal for all of about five seconds. The moment Lou glances over her shoulder at me, the moment her heated gaze meets mine, I go rock hard again.

God help me. This is going to be the longest fucking dinner in the history of time.

3
LOU

We're married. I can't believe it.

I spread my fingers and look down at the ring on my hand. Dinner went by in a blur, and now that we're back in our room, the whole thing feels a little like a dream.

"Beautiful," Ward whispers behind me.

"It is, isn't it?" I say, letting the simple gold band catch the light.

He grabs me so quickly that I don't have time to do anything but squeak as he scoops me up in his arms.

"You know I wasn't talking about the ring," he says into my hair, and I can hear the grin in his voice.

I tilt my face up and kiss his neck. "Yes, I do."

He carries me over to the bed. We've just put Ramona down for the night, and that means we've got some business to continue. Ward lays me gently on the comforter and lowers himself beside me. There's a devilish look in his eyes and one side of his mouth is raised in that lopsided smile of his. Some of his auburn hair has flopped across his face, and he pushes it back with one hand. Despite his urgency back in the dining room, he doesn't seem to be in a hurry right now.

"Do you remember our first time?" he says, still grinning as he reaches out and grabs one of my curls in his fingers.

"I do." It was out in the maze, almost exactly the spot where we just said our vows. I shiver as the memory comes back. Until that night, I'd never known anything like the pleasure I experienced with Ward. It changed me. It *still* changes me, every time we come together.

"That was it for me," he says. "After that night, there never could have been anyone else for me."

"Or me," I whisper.

He props himself up on his elbows above me, and though his grin has fallen a little, the way he's looking at me now makes my insides twist. I let my eyes slide down his body. He's always made me feel so small, so delicate, and never more so than when he holds his hard, muscled body over mine, the way he's doing now.

"I mean it, Lou," he says. "If anything ever happened to you... that would be it. I don't think I could go on."

My heart flutters as his face drops close to mine.

"I'd die too if you were ever taken from me." His lips brush against my cheek. "And then I'd find Death and fight him for you."

I laugh softly. There's no doubt in my mind he'd

do just that.

"I'm yours in life and in death and anywhere beyond," I whisper, running my hands up his back. "But I don't want to talk about death tonight."

He pulls his face away from mine again, and some of the humor has returned to his eyes. "I can agree with that. There are definitely a few earthly pleasures I wouldn't mind enjoying right now." He grinds his hips against me.

I groan and dig my fingers into his back. "I've been waiting all night for this."

"You have no idea," he says, his voice practically a growl as he hauls himself back and undoes his belt. "I was hard as a fucking rock all through dinner."

"Mm. Then maybe I can help you with that." I shift beneath him, repositioning myself so that he rests between my thighs. And then I grab his face and pull him down into a kiss.

I will never tire of Ward's kisses, not for as long as I live. Every one is like a new breath of life, like a shot of energy and hunger straight into my bones, and I open my lips beneath his, ready to take everything he has to give me. My hands tangle in his hair as his mouth sinks down on mine.

He groans against my lips. His hands are tugging at my dress, trying to pull it up my legs—which isn't entirely effective, considering I'm stuck beneath him. Normally I'd let him take his time, but tonight, I don't have the patience. I need him now.

I wrench my lips away from his. "Roll off me for a second. I'll need your help getting out of this dress."

He props himself up slightly, but he doesn't get off me. Instead, he shakes his head, that wicked grin stretching across his face again.

"Oh, no," he says. "You're not getting out of this dress. Not yet."

He moves his hips just enough to allow him to pull the skirt up my legs. Though it's summer, the air feels strangely cool against my bare skin, and I quiver slightly as he lets his fingers trail up the inside of my thigh.

"I've spent all evening imagining the things I'm going to do to you in this dress," he says. His blue eyes have darkened, and there's a rough quality to his voice that wasn't there even a moment ago. "I'm planning to make sure it's good and properly used before this night is over."

"Are you, now?" I say.

His grin widens, but instead of teasing me back, he falls and attacks my mouth again.

I throw my arms around his neck and hook my legs—now free of the confines of the skirt—around his. One of his hands is still wedged between us, sliding up my inner thigh, and I gasp against his mouth as his fingers slide across the lacy undergarments I bought especially for tonight.

We're married. It still feels so surreal. I never could have imagined my life would be like this, that I'd end up here—especially after some of the things I've been through these past few years. I didn't know who I was. What I wanted. But now I do—I'm Ward's wife. Ramona's mom. I'm here to love them and protect them. To give them everything they need. To be the best version of myself for them.

That is what Ward has given me—he's taught me who I am deep down inside. Before him, I always felt like I was playing a role—first I was the rich Cunningham daughter, then the selfless volunteer on the other side of the globe, and then, most recently, the wild fugitive. Heck, I even made up a false identity to get a job at Huntington Manor. My whole life was just one act after another, and never did I feel like I was ever just *me*.

Until Ward. With Ward I'm Lou, only Lou. I don't have to put on an act or pretend to be anyone else. I don't think I could pretend anymore, even if I wanted to. It's not just that he'd see right through it—which he would, without a doubt—but he just has a way of bringing out the truth. He has that sort of magic over me.

I tighten my arms and legs around him. He doesn't stand a chance—before he even realizes what I'm doing, I've rolled him over onto his back with me on top of him.

He doesn't seem to mind. He laughs and kisses me again, nipping at my bottom lip as his hand once again finds its way up the back of my thigh beneath my skirt.

My sound of pleasure is muffled against his lips as his fingers dig into me. One of his fingers slips beneath the lace of my panties, and I'm so distracted by his tantalizing touch on my bare skin that I don't notice his other hand drifting up my body until it's too late. His fingers slip beneath my arm and wiggle against my armpit.

I can't help it—I've always been ticklish, but Ward has it down to an art. He knows *exactly* where and how to touch me, and I burst into laughter as my nerves go haywire.

He's unrelenting. Now his other hand has joined in, tickling me wherever he can reach, and I'm helpless, twisting and contorting as I try to get away.

And laughing so hard I can hardly catch my breath.

"Ward!" I manage between laughs. "I'm... gonna... kill...*ahhh*!" The giggles take over again, and now he has me exactly where he wants me. He twists and rolls us both back over, returning us to our original position with him on top of me.

"Not... fair..." I protest, but I'm weak beneath his hands. He's laughing just as hard as I am, enjoying every minute of this, and I know I only have one line of defense.

I have to turn the tables.

He's ready for my attack, but not ready enough. My small hands slip easily beneath his arms, and soon he's nearly as helpless as I am. Our hands are everywhere, fingers wiggling, and we're both laughing so hard that the bed is shaking. Tears start to leak out of my eyes.

Finally, I see an opening again. I hit just the right spot on him, and that gives me the opportunity to push him over once more onto his back. Then I pin him down.

His hands immediately go to my waist. He's stopped tickling me—instead, he grips me firmly at the hips.

I stop, too. My chest is heaving as I sit up, and between my legs his own body rises and falls heavily as he tries to catch his breath. For a moment, we just stay like that—me straddling him, him gripping me, both of us staring into each other's eyes as we gasp in mouthfuls of air—and everything seems to still. My heart pounds in my ears. Ward licks his lips.

I love this man so much it hurts. Hurts *physically*— and not just from laughing too hard.

I lean down slowly, never breaking his gaze. Much

of my hair has escaped its pins, and loose curls fall down around my face. The ribbon that Lily helped me weave through my locks dangles and drags across Ward's chest as my face gets closer and closer to his.

I love the scent of him—of his breath, of his sweat, of his hair—and I inhale deeply as I close that last space between us. His hands tighten on my waist, but otherwise, he doesn't move. Instead, he waits for me.

The first brush of my lips against his is light, delicate. The second is a little deeper. The third, deeper still. He returns my kisses, but he doesn't try to take charge. Instead, he lets me lead the way. He matches the passion of my kisses but never pushes beyond what I'm giving.

I continue to give him pieces of my desire—a touch here, a whisper there, a lingering sigh of a kiss to his bottom lip—but never too much. If I let the full force of my hunger free, there will be no controlling it. Instead, like this, I can give him the truth of these beautiful feelings one kiss at a time. *I love you. I need you. You're everything.*

Finally, he moves too. One of his hands leaves my waist and drops between us, going once again for his pants. My mouth continues to caress his one kiss at a time. *I love you. I'm yours. Take everything.*

I rise up on my knees, letting him slide his pants down slightly. And then he grabs my lacy underwear and tugs it aside, pulling the crotch out of the way as his other hand guides me gently back down.

He fills me perfectly. My breath catches in my throat as he buries himself, and I sink onto him as deep as our current position allows. My lips fall on his again, and for a moment we both freeze, our mouths pressed together, our breath mingling as our bodies react to the wonder of our joining.

I kiss him once more—*I love you*—before sitting up. My hands come to rest on his chest, and he grips my hips again as we start to move together.

The motion is soft at first—like a rolling wave—and I feel like we're both holding back on purpose, letting everything build, afraid to lose the intensity of emotion beneath the strong tide of lust. Our eyes are locked together, and even our breath seems to come in unison.

But slowly, bit by bit, we move faster. The hunger threatens to take over. Our bodies begin to lose patience and the yearning for pleasure starts to drown out everything else. We're still mostly clothed, and suddenly I *need* to be touching his skin. My fingers tear open the buttons of his shirt.

His hips are moving more vigorously, his fingers digging deeper into my waist. We're both gasping for air, and I can feel his heart galloping beneath my palms. It's nearly as fast as mine.

I rock on top of him, meeting every swell of his hips, reveling in the sweet fullness between my legs. There's no holding back the tide now.

We move together until I can't think or breathe, until I don't know anything but the intoxicating sensation of him moving inside of me again and again and again. And then all at once everything peaks, and I hear myself cry out as my head falls back.

Ward is only a moment behind me. He groans as he empties himself into me, and my body welcomes it. I want everything he has to give me.

When we both come down from the high, he pulls me down into his arms. I'm still straddling him, and he's still inside of me, but I don't want to move yet. Instead, I curl up against his chest and press my cheek against his. Our bodies still rise and fall in unison, our breath still in perfect rhythm.

"I love you, Lou," he murmurs into my hair.

"I love you, too," I whisper back. "My devilish husband."

He laughs and tightens his arms around me. "My angelic wife."

"So I'm the angel in this relationship?" I ask. Considering some of the things I've put him through—I wasn't exactly the saint the tabloids once made me out to be—I'm not sure I deserve that descriptor at all.

"You're perfect," he says softly. "And every day with you is heaven. That's enough of a reason for me."

Now it's my turn to laugh. "Don't start getting all cheesy on me."

"Mm, I think I'm allowed to be cheesy. At least tonight." His hands rise to my hair. "You look so beautiful. I just can't get over it."

"And you—"

My words are cut off by a sudden shriek coming out of the baby monitor. Apparently Ramona has woken up—and she doesn't sound happy.

I let out a soft laugh and let my head fall again. For most of Ramona's life, she's actually been a pretty good sleeper—or at least better than I was led to expect a baby would be. But I'm not going to lie—some nights have been hell. You never really know when you're going to get a good night's sleep or when you're going to be up every other hour tending to a crying child.

"Let her cry herself out," Ward says, still playing with my hair.

"Mm," I agree. We've been trying not to coddle her too much, but I'll admit that it's still insanely difficult to hear my daughter cry and choose not to do anything about it. I would do anything in the world for her.

"At least she didn't wake up ten minutes earlier," Ward says, and though my face is still buried against his neck, I can hear the smile in his voice.

I smile in turn, snuggling my face closer to him. "I'm not sure I even would have heard her."

We continue to lie there, nestled in each other's arms, as we wait for Ramona to scream herself out again. But though on some nights that strategy works, it doesn't look like we're going to be that lucky tonight.

"I'll go check on her," I say, sitting up slowly. It feels like I'm losing something, pulling away from his arms, but I'm not sure I can bear to listen to sweet little Ramona's cries any longer. Every sob tugs at my heart.

"No," Ward says. "Let me."

"But—"

"You checked on her last night. It's my turn." He sits up beside me and drops a kiss on my cheek before disentangling himself. "Besides, I want you ready and rested for when I return."

My lips curl up as I watch him climb off the bed. He tugs his pants up and shoots me one last grin before heading down the hall to her room.

I love this man. I love him so much that every part of me aches.

I grab the baby monitor and flop back on the

pillows, listening as Ward—my *husband*—enters our daughter's room.

He still sings to her every night when we put her down. And he sings now, lilting a few bars of a lullaby as he tries to comfort her. Some of his songs are ones his mother sang to him. Others are ones he's made up. A lump rises in my throat as I listen to him through the baby monitor. Little by little, Ramona's wails start to trail off.

I place the baby monitor back on the nightstand. Ward doesn't know anything yet, but I've been planning a surprise for him. We decided several months ago not to worry about having a honeymoon—between Ramona and the ongoing renovations here at the estate, it seemed impractical, especially considering we wanted there to be as little fuss around our wedding as possible—but over the past few weeks, I've been rethinking my position on the matter. Ward's made a couple of comments this summer about wanting to visit the beach again—something he'd never done before he and I ran off together—and honestly, I miss being on the road with him. Our travels together were brief—and crazy and emotional—but our souls connected on that trip. And I've never stopped thinking about it.

I want to plan a trip for us. Something special to celebrate the next phase of our lives together. Ward has given me so much over these past couple of years—now I want to give him something memorable in return.

Ramona has stopped crying. I can still hear Ward singing softly, so he's probably making sure she's asleep again before he returns. I close my eyes and listen to the deep tones of his voice. This is everything I ever wanted—a man I love, a beautiful daughter, a place that finally feels like home. What did I ever do to deserve it?

Ward keeps telling me I'm his angel. That I'm perfect. It scares me, hearing that word on his lips. I'm not perfect. Not even close. How can I ever live up to such a word? How can I be the perfect wife to the man who deserves one?

Ward's singing has stopped, which means he'll return any second. I sit up, spreading my wedding dress back down around my legs. I don't know how to be perfect—not even close. But though the very thought brings a knot to my stomach, tonight, at least, I can show him what he means to me one kiss, one touch, at a time.

I love you. I need you. You're everything.

4

CALDER

I haven't been able to take my eyes off Lily all evening.

It's not just the way she looks in that dress—but I'd be lying if I said that wasn't part of the equation. Over the past several months, I've watched her body change and grow, watched her curves become curvier and her whole body evolve into something so beautiful I can hardly believe it. It takes my breath away, watching her glow a little more each day. Watching her get heavier and heavier with our child. With *my* child. I don't think I've ever been hungrier for her, and that means my present craving is all but unbearable.

She looks ravishing tonight. My sister let her choose the dress she'd wear at the wedding, and Lily decided on a gown in a dark red hue that draws my eye to every one of her irresistible new curves. I spent most of the ceremony with my hands curled into fists, fighting the urge to grab her and pull that dress off of her right then and there, my sister's wedding be damned. And now that dinner is over and we're back in our room, there's no one to stop me from doing just that.

Except myself.

As much as I'd love to spend my entire life just staring at her body, drinking in every inch of her, that's not the only reason my eyes were on her tonight. For all that I love the things pregnancy has done to her body, I can tell these changes have been hard on her, especially these last few weeks. My sister's pregnancy was challenging, I know, but Lily seems to be having a much more difficult time. I can see the exhaustion in her eyes. She tries to hide her pain and discomfort from me, but I've been watching her too long and too closely to miss the signs, even when she puts on a brave face. She's overjoyed at the prospect of this child, but the pregnancy is taking a physical toll, and she seems especially tired today. The shadows beneath her eyes are deeper than usual, and I didn't miss the tension beneath her smiles for Lou and Ward.

If I felt protective of her before, it's nothing compared to how I feel now. I've only ever wanted to protect her, to guard her from the world, and now that she's in this delicate state, now that she has the most precious of precious things inside of her, it's like a fever—a primal need that burns through me whenever I'm near her.

"Can I get you anything?" I ask her.

She has her back to me, and I push her hair over her shoulder so I can get to the zipper of her dress.

This has become a nightly ritual for us—me helping her undress. What started as an act of necessity as her body changed has become a sort of erotic dance—different from the mad tearing off of clothes that used to mark the start of our evening activities, but much more intimate. I lean forward and touch my lips to the base of her neck, and she shivers in response.

"I'm fine," she says. Her head rolls back slightly as I pull my lips away from her skin. "But I have something to tell you. I didn't get a chance to say anything to you before the wedding, but we have an unexpected visitor."

My fingers pause on her zipper. "What do you mean?"

She twists slightly, looking up over her shoulder at me. Under different circumstances, that look would have driven me over the edge, but she speaks before I have the chance to devour her.

"My mom is here," she says.

It takes a moment for her words to properly register. "Your mom? I thought she—"

"Abandoned me and my dad? Ignored all my attempts to contact her? Yeah. But she's here now. Just showed up here this afternoon."

I've had more than my share of family issues, and the entire situation puts me immediately on edge. Lily doesn't speak much of her mother, but the few things she's said haven't given me a particularly high opinion of the woman. And for her to show up here without any forewarning, to reappear in Lily's life without any concern for the emotional consequences that might have on her daughter... well, it does little to change my initial assessment.

The look in Lily's eyes right now—the confusion

and stress this is causing her during a time when she needs as little of each as possible—cements my feelings on the matter.

"That woman has no right to walk back into your life," I tell her plainly.

"I know," she says, rubbing her cheek. "I know, I just... I couldn't turn her away. She has nowhere else to go."

"After this long?" I say, trying to keep my tone even. "Forgive me, Lily, but that's a thin excuse from a woman who's been out of your life since you were a little girl." I grab her zipper again as I attempt to regain control of my temper. I want to pull Lily back into my arms—and then go kick *that woman* out of our home and back out of our lives.

"She said she was in a bad relationship," Lily says. "Apparently the guy took everything she had and she left him. She doesn't know what to do."

"So she brought all of her problems to your feet?" Her zipper is entirely undone now, and though my eyes are briefly distracted by the strip of bare skin I've just exposed, my mind can't seem to focus on anything but what she's telling me.

"I didn't know what to do," she says softly. "I know I don't owe her anything, but when she was standing there... She's my mom, Calder. I couldn't just shut the door in her face." There's a slight quaver in her voice, and though she's no longer looking at me, I don't have to see her face to read her.

"I understand," I say carefully. My arms move gently around her, and it takes all of my power to keep the tension out of my touch. "I just don't want you to worry about anything else right now. I don't want you to concern yourself with anything but staying healthy and happy." My hands slide up over her belly, cradling that beautiful bump, and I automatically find myself trying to sense the small, familiar movements of our son beneath my palms.

She leans her head back against me, sighing. "Do you really think I should be suspicious of her motives?"

I tighten my hold. I want to tell her that everything will be all right, that her mother's sudden appearance is a happy miracle, but I respect her too much to lie to her.

I press my cheek against the side of her head. "I think it's suspicious that she's walking back into your life right now, when she's down on her luck and you're living in an elaborate estate. Are you..." I pause. "Lily, it's been a long time since you've seen her. Are you certain this woman is your mother?"

She jerks out of my arms, so suddenly and with such violence that I nearly stumble back.

"Are you accusing me of not knowing my own mom?" she demands, spinning on me. Her eyes are sharp. "Or are you accusing her of being some sort of con artist? It's been a few years, sure, but I know my own damn mom."

"That's not what I meant," I say. "I just think we need to make sure we're examining this from every angle."

"And that means accusing my mom of... of trying to take advantage of me?" She starts pacing. "There are a hundred reasons why my mom might be here, and I... I..." Almost as suddenly, she stops again, pressing the back of her hand against her eyes. "It can't be like that," she whispers. "I hate her, but she'd never..." Her hand drops, and her eyes are wet with tears. "I'm sorry. I didn't mean to get so worked up..."

I step forward and pull her into my arms. Every moment that passes, I hate that woman more and more. "You don't have to apologize for anything. I shouldn't have been so blunt."

"No..." she says, sniffling and burying her face into my shoulder. "You only said exactly what I was afraid of." She sniffles again, then makes a half-strangled sound that's almost a laugh. "God, I miss the days when I wasn't crying every two fucking seconds."

"You have every reason to cry." I run my fingers over her hair and try to ignore the way she smells. God, she's crying in my arms and I'm half hard already.

"Why did she have to show up *now?*" she whispers against my shirt. "Why couldn't she have waited until after the baby was here? Or just leave us alone altogether? Not that I don't want to see her... I mean, I know if I want to see her. I don't know how I feel about any of this. But she's my mom. Am I an idiot for letting her stay here?"

"No," I say against her hair. "You're a woman with a kind heart." My hand skims up her back, and I remember too late that her zipper is undone. My cock throbs at the feeling of her soft, bare skin beneath my fingers, but I don't let my touch linger there long.

She turns her face so that her lips brush against my neck. I shift my weight slightly so she won't feel the growing bulge in my pants.

"I really want to believe that she has a kind heart, too," she says. "But I don't want to be naïve."

"You're not being naïve," I say. "In fact, I think

you're handling her sudden arrival quite well, all things considered. Certainly much better than I have ever handled the sudden arrival of various family members." First Lou's arrival on the night I proposed to Lily, and then later the appearance of the possible half-brother we never knew we had... no, I'm definitely not very good at handling these things.

She tightens her arms around me. "Do you think I'm doing the right thing?"

"I think it's the best option considering what we know now," I say. If it were solely up to me, I'd have the woman back out on the street in a heartbeat, just for getting Lily all worked up, but I also know that doing such a thing would break Lily's heart. "We'll figure this out." *And I'll be watching your mother like a hawk.*

Lily nods, and the motion makes her lips press against my neck once again. My body responds instantly, and my fingers dig into her lower back. She lets out a sound that's halfway between a sigh and a moan, and I feel her press closer.

"Let's just forget about her for tonight," I murmur into her hair. Finally, I allow my fingers to travel back up her back, to brush against that bare strip of skin where her dress is undone. She groans deep in her throat, and that's all I need to hear. I turn my face and let my mouth skim across her ear, then down to her neck. My hands grab the pieces of her dress and pull it slowly off her shoulders.

"I've wanted to tear this off of you all night," I say.

"That would've made for a very interesting dinner," she says, a touch of humor returning to her voice.

"Indeed," I say, so desperate for her that I can

hardly think straight. Her mother be damned. *Everything* else be damned. I won't be content until I've devoured every inch of her.

I release her and slowly step around her so that I'm standing behind her once again. Her dress slides down her chest, and I unhook her bra, exposing her breasts. *God, those breasts.* Lily's breasts were always exquisite, but their new fullness makes them a work of art. They're glorious. Breasts it would take an entire lifetime to worship properly. And they've been much more sensitive since the changes started taking place. Sometimes all it takes is a single touch and she's trembling and moaning in my hands.

I give her more than a single touch right now. I slide both of my hands around her, letting one drift across each breast, spreading my fingers to hold as much of her as I can. I don't stop until I can feel the hard bud of a nipple at the center of each of my palms. And then I slowly tighten my grip.

Lily sucks in a sharp breath, arching against me. Her breasts press even harder against my palms, and her head rolls back against my shoulder.

I was afraid that as Lily's body changed she might be less inclined to indulge in physical pleasure—not because of any particular self-consciousness perhaps, but rather because of the discomfort and physical strain these changes are causing her—and while I would have respected her needs, I'm not sure how I would have endured it, not with my increased desire for her. If anything, though, pregnancy has made Lily even hungrier, and her desire runs as deep as mine. God, we've never known pleasure like this. Every time I make love to her, I learn new things about her body. Find a new place that makes her moan. We've discovered each other over and over again as her body has changed.

I kiss her gently on the side of her neck as I finally release her breasts. My hands fall to her dress and push it down over the swell of her belly, letting it puddle on the floor at her feet. Then my hands follow course, sliding over the warm, smooth curve of her body. Her arms come up and her fingers move through my hair. I'm still sucking on her neck, and I give her a nip as I press my hips against her, letting her feel what her body does to me.

I know I should be gentle. The protective side of me never stops worrying for her, or for my son growing inside of her. But from the very beginning, she's insisted that she's no more fragile than she was before, and with my blood running hot like this, I'm happy enough to believe her.

"Get on the bed," I growl into her ear. "Now."

She pulls out of my arms and goes obediently over to the bed as I hastily pull off my tie, then my shirt, then my pants. By the time I'm bare, she's spread herself out on her side on the comforter, and the look she gives me from beneath her lashes makes my cock pulse. In a second, I'm on the bed next to her. Stretching out behind her. Throwing my arm around her and pulling her back against my chest. My fingers get another handful of one of her luscious breasts. My cock—which is so stiff it's causing me physical pain—slides between the cheeks of her soft round ass and toward the wetness between her legs.

I will never get enough of her softness. Of the way her body molds so perfectly to mine, no matter what size or shape she is. Her heart beats madly in her breast, and her breath is nearly as ragged as my own. I bury my face in her hair and breathe her in as I shift my cock, pressing it right against her slick opening. She lifts her leg and hooks it back over mine, giving me easier access. But I don't push forward, don't do anything but tighten my grip on her swollen breast.

"Not tonight," she says, reaching back and burying her fingers in my hair. "Don't tease me tonight, please."

Normally I'm only too pleased to torture her right to the brink, but hearing her beg me like that—with that quaver in her voice—undoes me. There will be no teasing tonight. I can't deny her.

I can't deny myself.

With one push, I bury myself inside of her. She gives a little gasp as I fill her, and her body contracts around my cock. God, there's nothing like the feeling of being so deep inside of her, of feeling her warm, sweet muscles tighten and grip me.

I slowly withdraw, and just when I think I can't bear it any longer, I drive into her again. She gives another little sound of pleasure, and my fingers shift on her breast, moving to her nipple. When I pinch that smooth, hard pebble between my thumb and forefinger, that cry of pleasure becomes a moan.

My hips move, building force with every stroke. Again and again I drive into her, pushing my hips against her full, round ass, enjoying the sound of our bodies moving together almost as much as I enjoy the whimpers and gasps coming out of her lips. My fingers continue to toy with her nipple. In time, I'll move them lower and tease that sweet little clit of hers, but for now, I want her to keep making more of those intoxicating little sounds.

"Calder…" she moans.

My face is still in her hair, buried in her scent, but I shift and let my lips close around her ear. Just a nip, just to hear her squeak.

"I love you," I murmur into her ear. "My delicious, beautiful, intoxicating wife." *Wife.* Since the day we were married, I haven't been able to get enough of that word. She's mine. She'll forever be mine. And now we're having a child together, a son created of her and me—something beyond *us.*

My hand finally releases her breast and slides down to her belly, the physical proof of our love. Of her bond to me, and mine to her. *I* did this to her. I made her body grow and change. Made my claim on her visible for all to see.

Her fingers dig into my scalp, and I growl and increase the speed of my thrusts, pushing into her sweet, tight body again and again. My hand moves lower and dips between her legs, finding the hard bud hidden there. This time, the sound she makes is deeper, throatier, and her tender body arches against my hard one.

I'm close. My whole body is taut with it, and my cock most of all. But I won't have my release until I've given Lily hers. I press and rub and tease her clit, drawing whimper after whimper from her lips. Our bodies have found their rhythm, our tangled legs bending together, my hips and her ass meeting with perfect friction.

I'm about to burst. God, I can hardly restrain myself anymore. My teeth close around her earlobe again. My fingers between her legs squeeze her until she releases a groan that sounds almost pained.

"Let go, Lily," I growl against her skin. "Come for me."

She whimpers, and I can feel her body stiffening, straining against mine. She's almost there.

"That's it," I rasp. "You're so close, my little minx. Come for me. Give it to me."

She cries out, finally finding her release. Her body tightens, and her slick passage pulses around my cock, tightening and bringing my own release rushing forward. I growl as it comes, locking my pelvis against her as I fill her.

When I'm empty, all of the tension leaves my body. She's still pulsing around me, and I bury my face once more in the fragrance of her hair.

She's trembling in my arms, and everywhere our skin touches is damp with sweat.

"I love you," she whispers.

Something about her voice doesn't sound quite right, and I sit up slightly so I can look down at her face.

"You're crying." I turn her face toward me, my stomach tightening. "Lily, what's wrong?" These aren't tears of passion or love—something isn't right.

But she shakes her head. "It's nothing. I'm just exhausted."

And I can see that exhaustion in every line of her face, see the aches and pains of the day—both the physical and the emotional—spelled out on her features.

God, why couldn't I have controlled myself for one damn night? How could I put my own needs above hers?

"Did I hurt you?" I ask. Why wasn't I thinking? After those hellish cramps she's been getting, I should have been gentler. Should have asked her how she was feeling before tearing off her clothes.

"I'm fine, I swear," she says, trying to wipe her

tears away.

"No, you're not." God, she was on her feet for half the day—why didn't I think about that? I should have offered her a massage, not jumped on her the moment we were alone. "Lily, you don't have to pretend with me. You're carrying our child. The least I can do is make sure you're comfortable, damn it."

"I'm just tired," she insists. "Please, just lie back down. Please."

I don't move, but I force myself to let out a long breath. I can't bear to see her like this. *I should have done more. Should have just helped her straight to bed—she needs her sleep more than ever these days. And I should have put her more at ease about her mother.*

"Please," she says again. "It's just been a long day. Just lie back down and hold me. Please."

I can't deny her, not when she speaks to me like that. But though I stretch back out beside her and pull her once more against my chest, my concerns don't leave me.

She might pretend to be strong, but she's struggling—struggling with pain and discomfort, struggling with exhaustion, struggling with all the changes that her body has endured. Now that she has her mother to deal with, she's struggling with her emotions, too. And she's trying to handle all of it by herself.

"I'm here," I whisper to her. "I love you, Lily."

And I'm going to do everything in my power to protect her, no matter what the consequences.

5

LILY

For the first time in over twenty years, I'm having breakfast with my mom.

It's still so weird—seeing her here, sitting across from me at the table, eating cereal and toast like this is completely normal. It's not normal at all.

But I guess, if I'm being completely honest, there's a part of me that finds it all frighteningly familiar. I thought I'd buried most of my memories of my mom, but they've all come rushing back, one after the other, and some are so vivid it's almost as if no time has passed at all. It might have been yesterday, the pictures are so clear—I see her making breakfast for me and my dad with her curlers still in her hair, her floral pajamas covered by a polka-dotted bathrobe I got her as a Christmas present. She somehow always managed to burn the eggs, but she made up for it by making little sandwiches out of the toast.

I study her across the table, and my chest tightens when I realize she still eats her toast in the exact same way—she's just layered two slices with strawberry jam and pressed them together. She takes a bite without looking at me, and I quickly glance back down at my plate. This is the strangest *deja vu* I've ever experienced in my life, and I'm not sure how I feel about it.

It's not exactly the same, though, I tell myself. Her style's a lot different, for one thing. The woman I remember wore classic but simple clothes—when she wasn't sporting polka-dotted gifts from her daughter, at least—while the woman in front of me looks like she never met a bright pattern she didn't like. Today she's wearing a dress with a turquoise and coral paisley print, and she's somehow found a coral lipstick to match. She has several beaded bracelets on each wrist, and a turquoise pendant hangs around her neck. I don't even know what to think about this style evolution.

But if I'm weirded out by my mom's presence here, I'm not the only one. The atmosphere here at the breakfast table is certainly different today—not *tense*, exactly, but definitely awkward.

I glance down the table. Lou is helping Ramona eat her breakfast. Ward seems happy enough as he munches on his eggs and bacon—he's been practically bursting at the seams with smiles since the moment he and Lou were married last night—but he's quieter than normal. Of course, there could be a lot of reasons those two aren't particularly chatty this morning. I mean, I can't imagine either of them got much sleep last night. Both of them were extremely pleasant to my mom when I made the introductions this morning—and she was all smiles as she insisted that they call her by her first name, Michelle—but I can't read either of them well enough to know what they're really thinking about the whole situation.

Calder, at least, is easy for me to read. He's been watching my mom all morning, studying her when he thinks I'm not paying attention. I know he's still trying to figure out what to make of her, but though it's clear that he's not exactly thrilled by her presence here—and I don't blame him, not after the way I behaved last night—so far he's still made every effort to be courteous to her. I reach over beneath the table and take his hand. He glances my way, and I give him a warm smile before picking up my spoon again.

Unlike the rest of the family—who's enjoying a full breakfast spread this morning—I'm stuck eating oatmeal. Apparently I'm one of those lucky women who gets blessed with morning sickness well into her third trimester, and oatmeal is the only thing I've found that seems to stay down this early in the day.

"Honey," my mom says, "are you sure you're eating enough?"

It's strange, being mothered by her after all this time. I don't like it. I'm an adult now, and this woman doesn't know anything about me.

"I'll have a snack in a couple of hours," I tell her. "If I try to eat too much now, I'll just throw it up again."

Her coral lips purse. "You're still having morning sickness this late? What does your doctor say about this?"

"He said that it happens sometimes and that I have nothing to worry about."

"Well, I have some morning sickness remedies you

should try," she says. "I just want to make sure you're eating enough for the baby. And eating *good* things—a lot of women just eat whatever they like when they're pregnant, but a baby doesn't need a dozen glazed donuts or a big dish of chili fries. He needs nutrients."

Beside me, Calder has stiffened. "Lily's diet is fine. You can rest assured that she and the baby are getting exactly what they need."

"Oh, I didn't mean to imply she wasn't," my mom says with a smile and a wave of her hand. "I'm sure you make sure she's taken care of. It's just hard to turn off my motherly concerns."

"You didn't have trouble turning them off twenty years ago," Calder says, his tone flat.

Even though she walked right into that one, my mom's eyes widen. And Calder's grip on my hand is so tight that I know he's barely maintaining his temper.

"Why don't we just finish breakfast?" I say lightly. "We can talk more about Bubble later."

My mom turns her surprised expression on me. "Bubble?"

My cheeks redden slightly. I'm so used to calling him that that sometimes I forget how silly it must sound to other people.

"Calder and I haven't decided on a name for the baby yet," I tell her. "So he's just Bubble for now." And I'm starting to think he's coming to like that name, because he gives me a little kick.

"Well," my mom says, sitting back. "I suppose that's one way of doing things." She glances between Calder and me. "You really should try to decide on a real name, honey. You two don't have much time now."

Calder tenses up again, so I quickly try to diffuse the situation.

"Did you have a nickname for me when you were pregnant?" I ask before he can say anything.

"Oh, no," she says. "We decided on a name the moment we knew I was having a girl."

"You named me after your favorite flower, didn't you?" I say softly. A vivid memory rushes forward— the memory of working in my mom's garden with her, of listening carefully as she pointed out each and every bloom.

"And these," she said, "are Easter lilies. Aren't they beautiful? Lilies have always been my favorite." She looked down at me. "You were named after these flowers, sweetheart. That's how much I love them. And now they're your flowers."

I stepped closer, wanting to get a better look at the blossom that gave me my name. The Easter lilies were simple—they were pure white, with only six petals—and while they weren't nearly as exciting as the snapdragons or the zinnias or the other bright, colorful flowers, I still found them quite pretty. I reached out to stroke one of the petals.

"Oh no, sweetheart," my mom said. "You can't touch them."

My young brain had trouble comprehending this. "But you just said they were my flowers."

She smiled down at me. "They are, my girl. But that's why you shouldn't disturb them. They'll die faster if you touch them."

Bubble shifts and kicks again, drawing me back into the present.

"Oh, yes," my mom is saying. "I suppose I did quite a bit of gardening back then, didn't I? I'd forgotten all about that."

You'd forgotten where my name came from? I want to say to her. But I don't. She's trying, I can tell. This was never going to be easy.

Calder is watching me closely, but I pretend not to notice. I know what he wants to say to my mom, but I don't want any conflict, not today. So I say nothing, and we fall back into silence. I force myself to eat more of my oatmeal.

My mom continues to eat, too, but she's also watching us. She glances across the table to Lou and Ward, then turns her gaze to Calder, then finally brings her eyes back to me.

"So," she says. "I'd love to hear more about your work, Lily."

I mentioned my work briefly to her yesterday when I was getting her settled in her room, and it seems like a safe enough topic—at least a lot safer than discussing the baby. Calder has stopped eating completely, and I can tell from the look on his face that he's just waiting for an excuse to kick my mom out of the house. I don't want to give him one.

"I'm in charge of the new Barberville branch of the Frazer Center," I tell her. "It's doing great so far. Most of our art classes and camps have already sold out for the rest of the summer. And our initial grants and donations far exceeded what we were expecting, so we'll be expanding a lot of our programs this fall."

"That's wonderful," my mom says, but I can't tell if her coral-lipped smile is genuine. "Is your dad working there too?"

I stiffen. I didn't get the chance last night to call up my dad and tell him that the woman who abandoned us was back. Honestly, part of me is secretly hoping that she might leave again before I have to deal with any potentially awkward situations.

"No," I say, trying to sound casual. "He still runs the original location. I'm completely in charge of the Barberville branch. He'll stop in every couple of weeks to check in on things, but I manage the day-to-day operations and all of the major decisions for my branch." I refuse to offer her any more information than that about my dad, but even if she wants to know, she doesn't press that particular point.

"I hope you aren't working too hard, not in your condition," she says.

Calder's hand tightens on mine again, but he leaves this one to me.

"I cut back on hours this month," I tell her as evenly as I can. "And I'll be taking a month of maternity leave when the baby arrives."

"Only a month?"

"I don't think I can give up work for longer than that," I say honestly, resting my hand on my belly. "Calder and I are still discussing the details, but he works from home at least three days a week. And I can always bring the little one to work with me in a pinch. I run the place, so I can make whatever rules I like. I don't think anyone there will be bothered by a baby."

"I think you're underestimating the amount of work a newborn can be," my mom says. "You're being entirely too optimistic. You're going to be exhausted all the time. Your brain will feel completely scrambled. You're not going to want to work—and you're not going to want to leave your child at all. And that's not even taking into account some of the finer details—have you thought about how long you plan to nurse? You *are* going to breastfeed him, aren't you?"

She's charged past the polite questions and into the personal ones now, but thankfully, Lou comes to my rescue.

"Lily and Calder have us to help," she says cheerfully, looking up from Ramona. "We've all lived here together since before Ramona was born, so they already have lots of experience with a newborn."

"It's hardly the same thing when it's someone else's child," my mom says. "Lily, I'd recommend at least three months of maternity leave, possibly even more. You might not realize it now, but it's hard work balancing a child with a life of your own."

"Which is why we all help each other," Lou says. She shoots me a small smile. "Lily has plenty of support here."

My mom doesn't look convinced, but at least she takes the hint to drop the subject. She lets a few moments of silence pass before she speaks again.

"I've been wondering," she says, setting the crust of her toast back on the plate, "what exactly *is* the living situation here? I'm a little confused. Who exactly owns this estate?"

Calder's grip is like steel on mine, and even Lou looks like she feels a little awkward. I know that from the outside the whole thing does look a little odd, but it works for us. This house is huge, much too large for one or two people to maintain on their own. And each couple has their own space—Calder and I have our rooms in one wing, Lou and Ward in the other— which gives us all more than enough privacy while also allowing us to still help and support each other like close family.

But I'm not sure the woman in front of me

understands family at all.

It's Ward that finally speaks. "This place is home to all of us. That's enough."

Technically, the estate belongs to Ward. And now Lou, I suppose, by marriage. That's always been a bit of a sore spot for Calder—this was *his* estate first, and now we're more or less living here because of the generosity of Ward and Lou—but I believe that even for him, the benefits of this arrangement far outweigh the downsides. Calder has always been proud of where he came from, and losing this estate—because of his father's irresponsibility, not his own—wounded him deeply. But if there's anything these last couple of years have taught us, it's that we have the power to make and create families and homes, even when life tries to take those things away from us. When I look into Calder's eyes, when I see the way he looks at me, I know in my bones that he'd never choose anything else but the path that led us here.

But now that we have a wonderful family we've created together, I'm still not sure what to do with the extra piece that has suddenly been thrown back into my life—a piece that now looks expectantly at me from across the table.

"Why don't I give you a tour later?" I tell her. "I'm not going back into work until tomorrow, so I have some time."

"I'd love that," she says. She plasters on a smile, and for now, the fact that she's *attempting* to play nice is good enough for me.

Calder is watching me out of the corner of his eye, and I give his hand one final squeeze before releasing it. I know he's worried about me—and about the woman across from us—but I'm figuring this out.

Taking her on a tour will accomplish two things—first, it will give me the chance to press her for more information about why she's here, and secondly, it will keep her away from the rest of the family for a little while. I need to show Calder that I have this under control.

But that doesn't keep him from cornering me when I go to freshen up after breakfast.

"Do you want me to come with you?" he asks.

I shake my head. "Thank you, but I think I need some time alone with her."

He's silent for a long moment, then finally says, "Are you sure about this?"

"Sure about what, exactly?" I say. "She's my mom, whether I like it or not. There's no changing that fact. I'm just figuring out how to deal with it."

His jaw is tight. "If you don't want her here, just say the word and I'll escort her out myself. You're under no obligation to her."

"She's my *mom*. I have every obligation to her."

He places a hand on each of my cheeks and lifts my face toward his. His dark eyes bore into me.

"You're under no obligation to her," he repeats. "She might be your mother by blood, but that woman was quick enough to abandon her responsibilities to you and your father. You owe her nothing."

Tears burn in my eyes. "She's still my *mom*. And just because she abandoned her responsibility doesn't mean I should. That would make me no better than her." I pull out of his grip. "I thought *you* of all people would understand that."

He presses his lips together, and the look in his eyes is so intense that it makes me want to shrink away.

"Your wellbeing is my first concern, Lily," he says. "I don't care who this woman is—if she's causing you distress, I don't want her in your life."

"Sometimes you can't avoid distress."

"And sometimes you can. Sometimes you should." He steps close again. "Lily, these past few weeks have been difficult for you—"

"It's just some aches and pains. I can handle it."

"You're exhausted, and not just physically. You need to take care of yourself, Lily. For the baby—"

"Are you honestly accusing me of not caring about the wellbeing of our child?"

Something flickers in his eyes—he knows he's gone too far. He clenches his fists and takes a step back, clearly trying to control himself. Slowly, the fight fades out of his eyes. He lets out a long breath.

"You're not going to budge on this, are you?" he says.

I shake my head, trying to calm my own frazzled emotions. "I don't know. I don't know what I'm doing. But I want to talk to her a little more before I make any drastic decisions." My eyes fall to my belly. "Tell me, what would you do if Taran Harker walked back into our lives again?"

At the mention of his and Lou's possible half-brother—it was never officially proved one way or the other—Calder stiffens. I know there are a lot of lingering questions—not to mention emotions—surrounding that man, but I know this is the only way I'll get Calder to understand.

"I'd hear him out," he admits after a moment. "I'd be willing to let him say his piece this time." He pulls me closer. "But if I thought he was a threat to you in any way, I'd cut him out of my life in a heartbeat."

"My mom is not a threat," I whisper.

"She's causing you stress at a time when you should be focused on your health. That *is* a threat, whether you want to admit it or not." His eyes flick down to my stomach before shifting back up to my face. "If she's sincere about wanting to be a part of your life again, then you don't have to do this now. You can wait until after the baby is here."

His concern makes my stomach twist, and though I hear the logic in his words, my heart won't let me turn my mom away—at least not until I've talked to her a little more. It might be a stupid decision, but at least I'll be able to sleep at night. I won't abandon her the way she abandoned me.

"You don't always get to choose your family," I say softly. "And like it or not, she's our family." Bubble presses against my belly, apparently agreeing with me. "If there's one thing I've learned in this life, if there's one thing *you* have taught me, it's that we should embrace the family life gives us. They might not be perfect, and maybe they've made some stupid, hurtful decisions... but they're ours. And sometimes they deserve second chances."

He dips his face closer to mine, and his breath washes across my lips.

"You're a much better person than I am," he murmurs.

"Not everyone can have a heart as dark and twisted as yours," I tease, my voice nearly as soft as his.

I glimpse a hint of amusement in his eyes in the split second before he kisses me. And then I'm lost in the feeling of his lips against mine, in the passion and desire I feel in his body as he backs me against the wall. I know my mom is waiting for me downstairs, but I can't help but succumb to that kiss, at least for a second. I hate that my mom's presence has caused any tension between us. I want to chase it away, one kiss at a time.

"This twisted heart is having a few dark ideas right now," Calder breathes when we come up for air.

And God, I'd do anything to give in to them. But there isn't time.

"My mom is waiting," I say, though I'm sure it's clear from my tone that I regret that very, very much.

He kisses me again, and desire threatens to drown me. If I'm not careful, I'll forget all about my mom.

"I have to go," I tell him, pressing gently against his chest.

"Tonight, then." His hands skim over my breasts, and I let out a soft moan as my nipples harden beneath my shirt. "Tonight, we're going to do some very, very dark things."

"I'm counting on it," I say breathlessly. I force myself to slide out of his arms.

I don't look back at him. I know if I do I'll give in to the hormones and the desire and the crazy emotions, and I need to be strong for this tour with my mom.

But I can feel him watching me as I leave the room, and I smile to myself at the feeling of his gaze burning into my back. Whatever tension my mom has caused between us, I know exactly how to fix things tonight.

* * *

In spite of everything, I find myself enjoying the tour with my mom. It's been a long time since I've shown someone around this place, and I like watching her face light up with pleasure and surprise at the house's secrets. I remember how I felt the first time Calder gave me a tour. I wanted to hate him—after all, the only reason I came out to the estate in the first place was to demand the money the Cunningham family owed the Frazer Center—but even then, I was already falling under his spell.

Sometimes I still wonder what would have happened if that storm hadn't stranded me here. Fate works in funny ways.

I take my mom by some of the fancier bedrooms, the movie theater, the rooftop pool, the gallery—and in each room, I find myself recalling my history with Calder in those places. I don't share any of those stories with my mom, though—she's still practically a stranger, and my intimate memories with Calder are ours to keep—but she must notice the blood that has rushed to my cheeks.

"Tell me," she says as we walk down the corridor, "how's your sex life?"

I nearly trip, catching myself on the wall at the last minute. "Excuse me?"

"Your sex life," she repeats. "You and Calder have only been married for a year or so, right? I'd hope you two still have a healthy sex life."

"I'm not really comfortable discussing this," I tell her.

She glances over at me. "Come now, sweetheart—we're long past the days when a woman should feel ashamed of her sexuality. Have you two been having sex regularly throughout your pregnancy? I know some women experience a decline in their sex drive during that time, but I—"

"I'm *not* discussing this with you," I say. "Can we

just get back to the tour?"

She doesn't look very pleased by my reaction. "Honey, I'm just trying to get to know you a little better. I know we've got a lot to catch up on, but we can at least try to open up to each other, can't we?"

"Forgive me, but I still hardly know you. And that means I'm not ready to talk about my sex life with you. That's private." She starts to speak, but I cut her off. "Before you say anything, I don't want to hear about your sex life either." *Not with my dad or with whatever guys have come after.* God, the whole thought makes me feel sick to my stomach.

We've reached the spa, the place where Calder and I spent our wedding night—but God help me if I'm going to tell her *that*. I also have no plans to tell her about the secret passages behind some of the walls, or the dungeon of a basement, or any of the other places that have played significant roles in some of my sensual games with Calder.

Fortunately, she becomes quickly distracted by the beautiful blue and green tilework on the walls.

"This is gorgeous," she says, spinning slowly and taking everything in. "I can't believe you live here."

"Neither can I," I admit, grateful to be on a new subject. Sometimes it still feels surreal, calling this place my home. I never had dreams of living in a mansion. And I certainly never thought that after all of the things that happened at the beginning of my relationship with Calder that we'd end up here together.

"Don't take it for granted," my mother says softly—and for once, she sounds more sad than judgmental.

Something about her expression tugs at my heart. I

don't want this woman to have any sort of emotional pull on me, but in spite of my best efforts to guard myself—in spite of the anger and resentment that I still feel toward her—she does. God, she always will.

"Where have you been all this time?" I whisper. I meant to build up to this question, meant to prepare myself for it, but I can't hold back any longer.

Her eyes soften. "That's a very long story, sweetheart."

"This is a very big place," I reply. "And we still have all the gardens to see. There's time." It's hard to keep the emotion out of my voice, but suddenly I'm that little girl again, desperate for her mom's love. Desperate to know the truth.

Her perfectly rouged lips turn down, and there's no denying the sadness in her eyes now. She turns away from me again before speaking.

"I just needed more."

"More?" What I really mean is *More than me? More than Dad, one of the best and kindest men I've ever known?*

"It's difficult to explain," she says. "I don't think I can even put it accurately into words. I just… I'm not sure this is the best time to discuss this, honey."

When would be a good time? Another twenty years from now? Part of me wants to grab her and shake her and force her to tell me, force her to answer my questions, but I don't. I'm not a child anymore. I refuse to beg for the scraps of her affection.

And she doesn't elaborate, so I stay silent. Finally I continue the tour, leading her through the rest of the ground floor before taking her outside. All the while the questions continue to burn in my mind.

"I remember my garden now," my mom says suddenly, surprising me. "It's just been so long since I let myself think about it. But it's coming back." She inclines her head, and I find myself wondering whether her memories are as clear as mine. "You used to come out and help me sometimes."

"I remember," I tell her. "You taught me the names of all the flowers. And showed me the lilies." She even let me bury some of the bulbs, hiding them beneath mounds of rich, dark dirt. Sometimes I used to pretend they'd grow up into beanstalks or magical briars. It all feels like a dream now.

The woman in those memories feels like a dream, too. Nothing at all like the woman who stands in front of me now.

My hands are on my belly again. It's hard not to think about Bubble when I'm walking next to my mom. I haven't even met him yet and I already know that I could never, ever leave him. Not for any reason. Emotions well up inside of me—anger and betrayal and a sadness so deep it brings tears to my eyes.

When I glance over at my mom, I see shockingly similar feelings reflected in her expression.

"Nothing I say can ever make up for what I did, I know that," she says softly. "But I love you, Lily. I never stopped loving you. I thought about you every day. And every night before I fell asleep."

I squeeze my eyes shut. I'm not prepared for this conversation. Not prepared to examine my feelings for her then or now. Bubble kicks, sensing my distress. I don't know what to say to this woman—*I hate you. I'll never, ever forgive you. Nothing you can say or do will ever make this right. I still love you, Mom. Do you really still love me?*—but none of the words come. Maybe I should have let Calder come along. Just having him near me gives me strength, helps me remember what true, unconditional love feels like.

He'd just get mad at her for upsetting you, I remind myself. *He'd only see the pain she's causing you. He doesn't care about her explanations.*

"Well, there's no reason to dwell on such things," my mom says lightly. "We're together now. That's what matters." I quickly open my eyes, but she's turned away—and when she turns back to face me, her smile is wide and bright again. "Tell me more about this husband of yours."

The sudden shift throws me. *She* might be able to shove those memories back down easily, but I can't— even though part of me desperately wants to.

I swallow, fighting back the achy feeling in my throat. There are so many things I want—*need*—to ask her, so many things I need to settle in my heart, but I'm still grateful for the excuse to put off that difficult conversation for just a little longer.

"Calder is amazing," I tell her. *Even when he doesn't understand what I'm going through.*

"He's very protective of you," she says.

That's putting it mildly. "He's protective of everyone he cares about. He's fiercely loyal. And stubborn— but in a way that makes me love him even more. He always fights for what he believes in. And for those he loves."

She nods and glances around. We've just reached the rose garden—in fact, we're standing on the exact place where Calder and I got married. Remembering that day brings even more emotions to the surface. I just love him so, so much.

"You love him quite a lot, don't you?" my mom says, stopping suddenly.

How does she do that? How does she guess exactly what

I'm thinking?

"Of course I do," I say, the emotion thick in my voice. "I love him more than anything. I'd do anything for him."

"And I don't even have to ask him to know that he'd do anything for you." She looks over at me. "I can see it in the way you two look at each other. Oh, honey, I'm so happy you found that kind of love. Most people aren't that lucky." She reaches out and gently touches a rose. "I've never felt that way for anyone."

In spite of everything, the regret in her voice makes me want to reach out and hug her—until what she's said fully sinks in.

"You didn't love Dad?" I find myself asking.

"Oh, sweetheart, I loved him. But not like you and Calder love each other."

I know this should sadden me, but instead, it's anger that rushes into my chest. "Then why the hell did you marry him?"

"*Language*, darling. And I married him because I thought I *did* love him. But I was young and foolish and had no idea what I was getting into."

I don't believe it. After everything...

"That's bullshit," I snap. "You made a commitment to him. You don't just jump ship because it gets hard. That's not how marriage works." Bubble picks up on my anger, and he gives me a particularly hard kick. "Love takes work."

"I wasn't happy, honey. I know that must be hard to understand in your situation, but I was lost. Your dad... he had a dream to build that arts center of his, and it was wonderful to see him do it, but he never got excited about me the way he did about his work.

And I… I felt like I had nothing. I had no dream like your dad. No great love. Nothing."

"You had me," I say, and I can't keep the bitterness out of my voice. I rub my belly, trying to soothe an increasingly agitated Bubble, but it doesn't seem to help. "And I don't know how you got the idea that Dad didn't love you, but you're crazy. You didn't see how he was after you left us."

It still brings a knot to my stomach to remember those days—while Dad tried to put on a brave face for me, even a young kid knows when her parent is in deep, heart-wrenching pain. I still remember the time, not a week after she left, when I couldn't sleep and crept down the hall to their bedroom—only to find my dad with his face in his hands, crying. It was the first time I'd *ever* seen him cry, and it shattered something inside of me. I was hurt and confused by what my mom did, but it was seeing how it affected my dad that completely broke my heart. The memory of him like that will be etched in my brain forever.

"I thought about taking you with me," my mom says softly. "But I didn't want to leave your dad all alone."

"Oh, so now we should be thanking you for your thoughtfulness?"

"That's not it," she says. "I told you, sweetheart, I don't expect you to forgive me. Or even understand. I just… as I said, I was lost. And confused. And I needed to find myself."

"And how did that turn out for you?" I don't care about keeping my temper anymore. Every word that comes out of her mouth is bullshit. The whole thing is making me queasy.

"I'm trying to make things right," she says. "I

wanted to make sure you were happy. That you weren't making the same mistakes I did."

"I *am* happy. Nothing in my life is a mistake. That doesn't mean I have it easy all the time, or that any of this is perfect, but it's mine and I love it and I work for it every day. And you know who taught me how to do that? Dad." I want to storm away, but my nausea is getting worse. Bubble's next kick hits me right in the rib, making me wince. "Don't you worry, *Mom*," I choke out. "I would never abandon my child. Not for any reason. I would never—*argh*." My insides tighten, and I nearly double over.

"Sweetheart?" My mom is at my side in an instant.

I bat her hand away. "I'm fine. Just give me a minute."

"How far along are you?"

I grimace as another pang shoots through me. *Was that a kick? Or something else?* "I'm not going into labor, if that's what you're asking."

"I just think we should—"

"I don't need your help!" I snap. "Not now, not ever." The worst of the discomfort has passed—I think. At least I don't feel like I'm going to be sick everywhere. "I've made it this far without you."

Her lips press together. I don't mean to be so harsh toward her, but right now it's hard to feel anything but anger for this woman. She's the last person in the world I want any advice from. *Just try to calm down*, I tell myself. *You're upsetting Bubble.*

"Why are you even here?" I ask her. "Do you just want to make yourself feel better? Or do you want something else from me?"

But I never get the chance to hear her answer.

6

LOU

I've never seen my brother this agitated.

For as long as I can remember, he's been so serious. So intense. He always wants to be in control, and it kills him when he can't—especially when something he cares for is on the line—but it's not normally this bad. All morning he's been pacing around the house, clearly on edge. I'm on my way outside with Ramona when I catch him in front of a window, staring out into the rose garden with his hands clasped behind his back.

"Spying?" I call to him from the doorway.

He's so intent on the scene outside the window that I startle him—he jumps nearly a foot at the sound of my voice. He runs a hand through his hair as he turns around.

"I'm not spying," he says. "I just don't like that woman."

"I don't think you're ever supposed to like your in-laws," I say, repositioning Ramona on my hip and coming to stand beside my brother at the window.

"I like Lily's father just fine. But then again, David never abandoned his daughter." There's a wrinkle between his brows as he looks back out the window.

I follow his gaze. Lily and her mother are out in the garden, and from their body language, they're not exactly playing chummy family right now.

My eyes shift back to my brother. He's changed a lot since Lily came into his life. In many ways, I think she's helped heal him—the way Ward has helped heal me—but on the other hand, he's never loved anyone or anything the way he loves her, and that does something to a man. It doesn't matter what Lily says—or what I say—he's never going to *not* worry about her, especially these days. I remember how Ward was when I was pregnant. If there's one thing that makes a guy go all crazy and possessive, it's watching his child grow inside the woman he loves.

But I can try to put his mind at ease, at least. I'm his sister. It's my job to call him on his crap.

"Lily's a grown woman," I remind him.

His frown deepens, but he doesn't look away from the two women in the garden. "Don't you think I know that?"

"Then you know that she needs to make the choice for herself whether or not her mom is in her life." I pull a bit of my hair out of Ramona's fist. "What exactly are you afraid of?"

"I don't trust that woman," he says, propping a hand against the glass of the window. "Why did she just show up out of the blue? What does she want from Lily? Family members don't just reappear unless

EMBER CASEY

they want something."

Whether or not he's making a reference to the night that *I* showed up at his apartment after our father died, I don't know, but I feel a small twinge of guilt anyway. A lot has happened since that night. But I'm not about to let Calder stand here stewing.

"What do you think she should do, then?" I ask him. "Tell her to go away? Cut her mom out of her life?"

"I never said that." He sighs. "Lily is far kinder than I am. And it's only natural that she should have a soft spot for her mother, no matter what the circumstances. But I don't want her upset over anything. Not right now. Not when…"

He doesn't have to finish that thought. We all know how difficult Lily's pregnancy has been.

But this is about more than just her pregnancy. Calder and I have both had a rough go of it since our father died—and had many, many family issues to deal with—but if anything, that's only made it easier to reconnect after we both decided to get over ourselves. Our family history gives us a certain understanding of each other that I'm not sure even our partners will ever fully understand.

"Have you had any word from Taran?" I ask him quietly, then wince as Ramona pulls on my hair again.

Taran Harker, our possible half-brother, showed up here last summer, right around the time when Calder and Lily got married. There was at least some evidence to suggest he might be telling the truth about his parentage, but after a fight in the garden with Calder—which resulted in Taran getting arrested—he apparently decided it was better to just walk away from our family. Even though Calder left him with an invitation to sit down and talk about everything like the adults we all are—no threats, no fights, no skulking about in the maze—it's been over a year and we have yet to hear from him. But that doesn't mean I don't still think about him sometimes.

Calder's face has softened a little. "I've thought about trying to find him and reach out to him again. But I don't know." He looks over at me. "He's as much your brother as he is mine. What do you think?"

"He's only our *alleged* brother," I say carefully. I've had this debate with myself many times. "We still have no real proof one way or the other, just a bunch of circumstantial stuff. And he didn't exactly go about contacting us in the most honest way."

"That's partially my fault," Calder says. "I didn't really give him the chance to speak with me."

My stubborn brother must be pretty worked up if he's actually admitting to being wrong about something.

"I don't want to cut him off completely," I admit. "At least—if he ever came around again, I'd want to talk to him. Hear more about his side of things. If life handed him the short end of the stick, if our father was a dick who abandoned his mother, it's not our fault—but it's not *his* fault either. If he's our brother, it's something we should all figure out together." Ramona has started sucking on her fingers, and I tilt my head down and plant a soft peck on her curls. "On the other hand, since we don't know the truth about him, we can't be sure of his motives. And if he's potentially a danger…" I look down at my daughter. "If it was just me—just *us*—I'd already be in the car, ready to hunt him down myself. But I have

Ramona and you have..." I look back out the window again.

"So you understand my feelings exactly," Calder says, jaw tightening.

"But if he's actually family... how can we let this go? If we sweep him under the rug, we're no better than our father."

"I gave him my number. Told him to contact me." For the first time in this conversation, Calder really looks at me. "If he wants to talk, he knows how to reach me. The ball is in his court now. I am *not* our father, Lou."

He's more like him than I know he wants to admit—but I won't point that out. I know in my heart that Calder could never, ever do what our father might have done—first of all, he'd die before he ever considered cheating on Lily. And secondly, he'd never abandon a child. I see the way he looks at Lily now, see how gently he touches her belly. I mean, only last year when I was pregnant with Ramona, he was *terrified* to touch mine. But the man I see in front of me is a man who'd die for those he loves.

"I didn't mean to suggest you were," I say.

He rubs his face. "I'm just so worried about her."

His voice sounds so raw that I find myself stepping toward him. This is about more than Lily's mother or our father. The strain of these last couple of months—of his deep concern for Lily—is really wearing him down.

"I know," I say. "But she's going to be all right. You won't let anything happen to her, and she knows that."

"She might know it, but she won't listen to me."

"Because if she listened to you, she'd be locked up

in a cushioned room all day, completely cut off from all the dangers of the world."

"At least she'd be safe there." One corner of his mouth tilts up slightly. "But I'm not that bad."

"You're pretty darn close."

That earns me a full smile from him. "I have every reason to be, I think."

"Yeah, you just try telling that to Lily. I'd love to see her reaction." I switch Ramona to my other hip. "I—"

Calder's hand hits the window, startling both me and Ramona—who blinks and then immediately starts wailing.

"Calder, what the heck do you think you're—" But now I've looked outside, seen what's happening in the garden. Lily has doubled over, her hands gripping her belly.

Calder doesn't respond to me. He rushes past me, and he's through the door in less than a heartbeat.

I rock Ramona in my arms, trying to calm her.

"Hush, baby girl," I say gently to her. "It's all right. Hush, my love."

But my eyes are back on the garden. If I managed to calm Calder at all during our little talk, I'm pretty sure it doesn't matter now.

Please let Lily be all right, I think. *And God help us all if she isn't.*

7

CALDER

I can't believe that after everything that's happened today, Lily is still being so damned stubborn. She gave me the scare of my life earlier, and while it turned out to be nothing this time, that doesn't mean we can just ignore what happened. Her mother upset her, then she experienced pain in her stomach. That's not just a coincidence. When we finally retreat to our room for the night, I tell Lily exactly how I feel.

"That woman needs to go," I tell her plainly. Her mother had some nerve showing up here in the first place, but for her to continue to put Lily through emotional turmoil is beyond acceptable.

"I'm fine," Lily tells me calmly—though how she can be the least bit calm after today absolutely confounds me. "I promise, Calder."

"It's not fine," I insist. "Lily, you have to be careful—"

"And that doesn't mean I have to avoid all difficult situations." She props her hands on her hips. "I never thought reconnecting with her was going to be easy. But if you're going to freak out every time things are a little difficult with her, then maybe—"

"I'm not *freaking out*," I tell her. "I believe I'm having a very understandable reaction regarding the emotional health of my pregnant wife." I move toward her, looming over her but not touching. "When I saw you out there in the garden…"

"Bubble was just feeling a little cramped, that's all," she says. "I'm okay now. I feel perfectly fine." She leans slightly toward me, but she doesn't touch me, either—we both hover right against the other without making contact. Her beautiful eyes shine with a challenge. She's not going to back down.

"You mean everything to me," I tell her. "You and this baby."

"I know," she whispers.

"It's driving me mad, not being able to protect you from this. If I had my way—"

"I'd spend all day in bed. And she'd be back out on the street. I know."

"Not on the street. But out of our lives until the baby is here."

"We don't always get to choose these things." She takes a step back, her hands resting on the round swell of her body. "While you were on the phone with the doctor, she talked to me a little more about why she came here. The man she was living with—he was awful. He literally took everything she had of value. All of her savings. Basically everything she had on this earth but the clothes on her back. She didn't have a lot of friends in her life—and those she did have were more loyal to him than to her. She couldn't turn to them. So she came here. She saw this as her chance to reconnect."

Has she forgotten that she's already told me what she and her mother were discussing in the garden? "So she decided that the best way to go about reconnecting was to explain that she didn't love you or your father enough to stay?"

"She didn't say it quite like that," Lily insists, but I can read the pain in her eyes, and I'm almost sorry to have repeated the words at all.

"I don't want you to get hurt," I say. God, she has no idea how helpless I feel. Every day I see the fatigue on her face, the strain in her eyes—and though I'm more than delighted by many of her body's changes, there's a part of me that aches every time I see how hard this pregnancy is on her. *I* did this to her. And I'll be damned if I don't do everything in my power to offer her comfort and protection, to guard her from harm.

But how can I do that if she's going to reject my help? If she's going to embrace the risks and turmoil even against her own better judgment?

She's stepped close to me again, and in her eyes I see a look I know too well—the look she gives me when she thinks *I* am the one being especially stubborn.

"I know you're just looking out for me," she says. "But I'm strong enough for this, I promise. You know why? Because of you." She reaches out and touches my face.

It's all I can do not to tug her into my arms. But this is a conversation we need to have—and I'm not about to let her slither out of it with gentle touches or that fluttery-lashed look. Oh, no. Not even this little minx can make me budge this time.

"*You* are the reason I can face her," she continues, pressing closer until her warm, round belly is right against me. "You've given me so much strength, so much support. I know that you love me and that you'll be here for me no matter what."

"I will be here for you," I begrudgingly agree, frowning slightly when I hear how rough my voice is. Even when I'm angry, this woman has complete power over me. "I love you more than anything, Lily."

"So you can see why I'm not worried about her. Yes, she brings up some complicated feelings. But at the end of the day, whatever happens with my mom, I know that you'll be here for me." She leans closer still, standing on her toes and tilting her face toward my ear. "You'll be there to take me in your arms and make everything all right again. You'll be there to kiss me until I forget about any of the pain, to torture me with your fingers and lips until I know nothing but pleasure again. Until there's no doubt that I am the most desired, most loved woman in all the world."

Her hands skim up my sides and then across my chest, finally coming to the buttons of my shirt. My body is responding even before she undoes the first button—sometimes even the simplest, barest touch from this woman can bring me to the edge of my restraint—but I grab her hands, stilling her fingers before she can go any further.

"Lily, we're in the middle of a conversation."

Her lashes drop slightly. "Then let's talk."

Her tone suggests that the kind of talking she has in mind is very different from what I'd like to do, and her fingers wiggle in my grip, trying to break free.

"We need to settle the issue of your mother," I say slowly, carefully. Because now she's biting her lip, teasing me, and my cock is trying very much to misbehave.

"Convince me," she says.

"There will be no convincing you in this mood, you stubborn little minx."

"Not with words, maybe."

Now her eyes are gleaming, and I know the cause is truly lost—at least tonight. But she doesn't get to win that easily.

"I'm not playing this game, Lily," I say.

"It's too late," she says, her lips curling up in a way that makes me throb against the fabric of my pants. "From where I'm standing, you're already playing."

She pulls her hands out of my grip, but rather than going for my buttons again, she takes a step back. She reaches up and pulls the tie out of her hair, letting the strands fall down around her shoulders.

"This isn't going to work," I tell her.

"Then we're just exactly where we started," she replies. "No harm done." She pulls her shirt up over her head, revealing her bare stomach and the large, swollen curves of her breasts spilling over the edge of her bra.

Even on the days when she's wearing simpler maternity clothes—things she can easily take off herself—I still consider it my duty and my pleasure to undress her. Which makes her current striptease all the more tantalizing—and she knows it.

She's already started sliding her skirt down. She does a little wiggle side to side as she shimmies the fabric over her hips—*God, that shimmy is enough to make a man's cock explode*—and then pushes it down her thighs.

Stay strong, I tell myself. *She's tormenting you on purpose.*

But then she reaches behind her back to undo her bra, a motion that makes those full, enormous breasts of hers swell and threaten to pop right out of their binding.

Who the fuck am I kidding?

In two strides I'm in front of her and her face is in my hands. My lips come down on hers and my tongue slips deep into her mouth.

Her hands slide up around my neck, which is exactly what I'd hoped might happen—no one but me is allowed to peel that far-too-tiny bra off of those intoxicating breasts. I reach around and undo the clasp with one hand.

I feel her smile against my lips, but she's a fool if she thinks she's won. I press my hands against her back, pulling her snugly against my body. As much as I love her current round shape, though, I'd prefer a little more contact for my hungry cock. But I'm nothing if not resourceful.

I twist her around, turning her in my arms until her back is pressed to my chest. It's a shame that it's nearly impossible to reach her lips from this angle, but there are still plenty of things to do with my mouth. I suck her earlobe between my teeth as I slide her panties down over her hips, leaving her completely bare in my arms.

"You've forgotten who gets to undress you," I growl into her ear. "That pleasure belongs to me and me alone."

She lets her head roll back onto my shoulder as

she releases a throaty laugh. "I'm yours to undress whenever you like."

"Don't think you've weaseled your way out of our discussion," I slide my hands up to her breasts—*God, I can't get enough of these breasts*—and weigh them against my palms. "We're going to have a nice long chat about your wellbeing."

"If you're so concerned with my wellbeing, then maybe we should stop," she says, her voice cracking slightly when I squeeze one of her nipples. "Unless you plan to be exceedingly gentle with me tonight."

Maybe I should. After last night, I promised myself I'd be more careful. But *gentle* isn't possible with Lily, not when she's getting me worked up like this. The temptress knows exactly what she's doing with me. God, my cock is throbbing in pain right now, and I still have my fucking pants on.

It takes all of my strength to peel my hands away from those luscious breasts, but I do—if I don't get these pants off now, terrible things are going to happen. I nip at Lily's neck as I undo my belt, and my arousal grows with every gasp of breath from her lips.

My pants are off. My shirt goes next. Then I wrap my arms around her and instead of moving us both toward the bed, I nudge her forward toward the wall.

Lily puts her hands out in front of her, catching herself against the wall as I press up behind her. This is another position that we've been playing with quite often since Lily started growing—and having her round ass pressed right against me never fails to make me ache. She leans forward, her loose hair falling down over her shoulders, and I position myself behind her, sliding one of my hands up her body as the other guides my cock between her legs.

My body is tense, already aching for relief, but I take my time sliding into her. She makes a sound of pleasure, and it pleases me to know that no matter how stubborn she might be, no matter how much we might argue, there is one thing that will always bring the same sweet sounds from her lips. One thing on which we will both always agree.

After that first slow stroke, the need overtakes me. She's just as eager, my dear sweet Lily—at least if the way she pushes back against me is any indication. Her cries are getting louder and throatier with my every thrust.

I suppose she is right, I think with a hint of amusement. *I can't be worried so very much over her wellbeing if I can't keep myself from taking her like an animal against the wall.* But if there's one thing I've learned during my time with this woman, it's that she can take the entire strength of my pleasure and my need—and give both back just as fully.

My hands tighten on her hips, and I grind against her until I'm nearly delirious with desire. When I feel her start to come, when her warm, soft passage begins to contract around my cock, I can't hold back any longer. I give one more hard thrust and fill her with my release.

Afterward, for a long while, we both just lean against the wall, trying to catch our breath. Our arms are tangled around each other and I can feel her heart racing beneath her breast.

"What were we arguing about?" she says dazedly.

I know—from her tone, if nothing else—that she has truly forgotten our argument in the haze of her pleasure, if only for the moment. And even if I believed she actually expected an answer, I wouldn't give one.

Because I haven't forgotten. No matter how many times she teases and seduces me, no matter what distractions fall in my path, nothing will ever make me forget the danger she's in—or keep me from putting everything on the line to protect her.

8

WARD

It's been over a year since I started renovating this place, but I think I've finally finished the south side of the house.

Lou's been teasing me this week, telling me that I should take a little time away from my tool belt—after all, we've only been married for a couple of days and it's not like we took a honeymoon—but honestly, I've never been more eager to get all of my projects done. To finish making this place ours. Now that we're officially a family, now that the responsibility is fully on my shoulders, I'm determined to give my wife and my daughter the best home possible.

Of course, considering the size of this place it'll probably take me about ten more years to finish, but who's counting? It's hard not to feel satisfied with the work I've done so far. We have big plans for this place—but our first priority is to get the house and estate back to what it was, to erase all evidence of Edward Carolson and Huntington Manor.

"What do you think?" I ask Ramona. Lou and Lily went into town today, so I offered to take Ramona for the afternoon. Normally I don't want my daughter anywhere near my renovation projects—there are too many dangers for a small child—but today I want to show her what I've done. How her mom and I are clearing the shadows of the past and building a life for her.

Edward Carolson—my biological father—wasn't a terrible person, I guess. But he wasn't really a good one, either. I didn't even know who he was until a couple of years ago, after he hired me to help develop this place into a luxury resort. He died before I had the chance to get to know him, but I have a feeling we wouldn't have gotten along even if we'd had all the time in the world. We were from different planets. He left me and my mother to live in poverty while he and his family had everything anyone could ever want.

Leaving me this place was probably his way of trying to make it up to me, but while I'm grateful for the comfort and security of this estate, it can never make up for what Edward Carolson didn't do.

I stroke Ramona's hair. Her curls are so soft beneath my fingers. Sometimes it still terrifies me, knowing that I have a kid. I have no idea how to be a dad. I didn't have one to show me the way. I mean, some of this stuff is common sense—give her love and attention, make sure she has food and clothing and clean diapers, protect her from outside harm— but in most ways, I still feel lost. I don't want to be a good father for her—I want to be *the best* father. And deep down, no matter what I do or how hard I try,

I'm deathly afraid I'm going to screw this up somehow. That I'm going to fail to be the dad that Ramona needs or deserves.

Lou says I'm crazy. She tells me I'm a great dad, but the fear still sticks. It's a knot in my chest that I feel every time I hold my daughter, every time I look down into her angelic little face. This is everything that I've ever wanted—a woman who I love more than life itself, a child we created from our love, a safe and happy home—but I'm not sure I deserve it. I mean, the only reason I have this house at all is because my asshat father felt guilty. I didn't earn any of this myself.

This is all too perfect, and somehow it's going to fall apart.

I take Ramona outside. She's only just woken up from her nap, so she's still a little groggy and quiet, but her wide eyes take in everything around us.

"Does it feel like home?" I ask her.

Ramona sucks her lip into her mouth and stares up at me.

I rub her back and smile. *My precious girl.*

"I'm thinking of reworking the stones in the courtyard on the eastern side of the house," I tell her. "But I have to talk to your mom first. She has some ideas for the garden."

I continue to walk down the gravel path, and Ramona twists her head around, trying to take everything in. She's reached an age where she's curious about *everything*—and since she's also starting to walk, I know the next few months are going to be a bit of an adventure.

"I don't think I've ever taken you on a tour of this place," I tell her. "Your parents have a lot of history here. We met just up there." I point to a window above us. "I won't tell you all the details about that, though."

I continue around the house, and Ramona perks up a little more. Pretty soon, she's gurgling and babbling in my arms.

"Da da!" she says. She raises her hand toward the sky. "Buh! Buh buh buh!" A flock of birds sweeps by overhead.

"That's right—birds," I say with a grin. "Birds."

"Buh buh!"

I laugh. *We'll have to work on that one.*

"We used to spend a lot of time out here in the maze," I tell her as the labyrinth comes into view. "This is where I fell in love with your mom. And where I proposed to her. And, as you might remember, where we got married." *Married.* Jesus, even just saying that word brings me joy—and anxiety. So much depends on me now.

"I'm doing my best," I tell Ramona—and myself. "I promise I will always do my best." But this still feels like uncharted waters. I mean, I never thought of living in a place like this. Never imagined I'd be this madly in love. Never even really thought about kids. I was always just fighting—fighting for more, for some little bit of happiness in a life I thought had screwed me over.

Fuck me, who'd have thought I'd become a rich, respectable man?

Being rich isn't exactly what I thought it would be. I mean, don't get me wrong—it's great. I wouldn't trade it for anything. Having this sort of security for my family is incredible. Let's be real, though—I'm not a billionaire or anything. Most of my wealth is tied up in this property—though Lou and I got a decent chunk of money by selling off supplies and furniture and other bits of Huntington Manor that we didn't want or need.

But I'm still getting used to feeling *safe*. Having money at my fingertips whenever I need it. Being able to work for fun, on projects I truly care about, instead of scrambling from paycheck to paycheck, always looking for that next gig to cover my rent for the month. Sometimes it feels like I'm living someone else's life.

And wealth comes with its own set of complications. After we got over our differences, I was happy to invite Lou's brother and his wife to move in with us. This house is way too big for just me and Lou and Ramona. Honestly, it was a little creepy living in such a huge, empty mansion by ourselves. Having other people here brings more life and energy to this place. And let's be blunt—all of us wanted and needed the support of family close by.

But I also feel like every long-lost relative and his brother has suddenly started creeping out of the woodwork. From the moment the news went public that Edward Carolson had left this place to me, I had old friends calling me out of the blue, asking for money. And let's not even think about that guy who showed up here last summer, claiming to be Lou and Calder's brother. I mean, he might actually be their brother, but people like that weren't stumbling into my life when I was barely making ends meet.

Now Lily's mom is here. I know we're supposed to be giving her the benefit of the doubt, but I'm pretty sure it's only a matter of time before she asks for money.

So yeah, things are different now.

"Da," Ramona says. "Da wa wa."

Wa-wa is her way of asking me to put her down.

"You want to walk?" I ask her, lowering her carefully to the grass.

I set her on her feet, and she clings to my leg. The sun shines off of her red hair as she twists her head, looking around her. She begins to bounce slightly, bending her knees up and down as she gets her bearings.

"Where do you want to go?" I ask her. "I'll help you."

She grins up at me, flashing her handful of baby teeth. "Da da!"

Jesus, this girl has me wrapped around her little finger. Yeah, I might still be getting used to the life we're building here, but I can't regret anything that led me to this.

Ramona finally decides on a direction, and she points a chubby hand away from me, toward the maze.

"All right," I tell her. "Let's go." I bend over and take her hand, then move forward a step.

She toddles after me on unsteady feet, then grabs my jeans again.

Step by step we move across the grass. She can't seem to build up the courage to do more than two or three steps at a time, but I'm okay with that. When this girl gets moving on her own, there'll be no stopping her—and I'm definitely not ready for that.

Jesus, how did you grow so fast? She needs to slow down. Give me a chance to figure out what the hell I'm doing—or the chance to build her the home she deserves.

I don't think I'll ever not feel a little restless in this place. Not when it was just handed to me. I know I should just accept that I got lucky—and looking down at my daughter, I'm pretty sure I'm the luckiest guy in the whole damn world—but I don't think I'll ever stop being afraid that it'll be taken away from me again. That's why I've been throwing all of my energy into renovating this place. I need to put my own stamp on this life. Pour my own blood, sweat, and tears into this estate. Give Lou and Ramona something I built with my own two hands.

But in the back of my mind, I'll always be wondering, *Is it enough?*

9

LILY

I'm not sure who is driving me more insane—my mom or Calder.

It's been a week since my mom showed up at the estate—but it feels more like a lifetime. I still don't know quite how I feel about her. Yes, she's apologized. Yes, she's shown some remorse. But I'm not convinced that, given the choice, she wouldn't do exactly the same thing again. She might be sorry that she hurt me, but is she sorry that she left?

It doesn't help that her continued presence here has put a strain on my relationship with Calder. I know he's only looking out for me, but damn it, if he isn't the most pigheaded man that ever lived. Just because I'm pregnant doesn't mean I need to be coddled. He needs to accept that I'm strong enough to deal with this.

At least that's what I tell myself. Sometimes I feel

my resolve melting, find myself thinking that he might be right—and honestly, it *would* be easier if my mom weren't around, and not just because she seems to have an opinion about *everything* in my life. She's put everyone on edge—even Lou and Ward, though they're too kind to say anything—with some of her tactless comments and questions. Maybe it's unfair to ask the others to accept her.

But then I look at her and I see the woman I once knew—the one who used to make me breakfast in her curlers and tuck me in with a story every night. In my memories, she's gentle, loving, giving. Where did that woman go?

She's hurting just as much as you are, I keep telling myself. *She's lost. She needs my help, and I'm in a position to help her.* I can't abandon her when she needs me the most. She just needs a little assistance getting back on her feet—and the sooner I help her do that, the sooner she's out of my hair.

Now I just need to make sure Calder doesn't murder her before we get to that point.

"Are you sure you don't want to leave her here with me?" he asks as I'm getting ready to head in to work. He's working from home today, but I have to oversee a couple of things at the Center.

"I'm not leaving her alone with you," I tell him.

"I just don't like the idea of you being stuck with her all day. And frankly, I don't even think you should be driving in this condition."

"We've had this conversation before," I say, crossing my arms. "As long as I can reach the pedals, I'm going to drive. I'm perfectly capable of operating a car in *this condition*. And as for my mom, she's already agreed that she'll make herself busy while I work. In fact, she was talking about using my computer to look for an apartment in Barberville."

I assumed he would see this as good news—after all, it would get her out of our home—but instead, his dark eyes sharpen.

"So she plans to make herself a permanent fixture in our lives?" he says.

"What else would you have her do? Move to a city where she doesn't know anyone?" I put my hands over my face, trying to calm my emotions. It's not even eight in the morning and already my body aches all over. I'm not in the mood for another fight.

I hear a step, then two, and then Calder's arms are around me. In spite of my anger, I let myself sink against his chest, burying my face in his shirt. Why can't we just forget everything else today and curl up in each other's arms?

"I'm sorry, Lily," he says against my hair. "I wasn't trying to upset you."

"Why do you insist on hating her?" I ask, my voice muffled by his shirt. It's an unfair question, but I don't care. I'm exhausted. Why is it that now, when I'm only a handful of weeks from becoming a mother, I feel like such a child? I don't know whether to blame the hormones or my mom or my own immature fears, but I hate it.

Calder lets out a sigh, his hand running up the length of my back.

"I don't hate her," he says gently. "But you have to remember, Lily, that I only know what I see." His fingers thread themselves in my hair. "I know that she left you and your father when you were quite young, and that it wounded you deeply. I know she returned here without warning, and with the barest of explanations. I know she keeps questioning you about your life and choices, even though she hardly knows you, let alone what might be best for you." His fingers still. "And, most importantly, I know that she's bringing you pain and confusion. I see it every day in your eyes, Lily, so don't try to deny it."

I cling to his shirt. "Don't ask me to make her go."

For a long moment, he doesn't say anything. And then, "You see the parts of her I don't. You have memories of her as a person you loved, and I see only who she is now. I understand that. But that doesn't mean I'm having an easy time accepting it."

"She'll be out of the house soon," I say into his shirt. "And then Bubble will be here and she'll be the last thing on our mind."

Despite everything, his chest rumbles with a laugh. "We really do need to come up with a real name for him."

"He'll be Bubble forever in my heart."

He laughs again as he pulls back, but when he looks down at me, his smile drops. In its place is a tenderness that makes my chest ache.

"Be careful today," he says, his voice rough.

"Don't worry. I'll be fine." I lift my mouth to his, kissing him goodbye.

He kisses me back, but the look he gives me as I leave tells me he doesn't believe things are fine at all.

* * *

It's obvious that my mom doesn't understand why the Frazer Center is so important to me and Dad, but she puts on a pleasant face as I show her through the facility.

"I'm glad you've found a job that makes you happy," she says. "But trust me—when the baby gets here, you're going to have to make some choices. You aren't going to be able to do as much as you're used to."

I know that on some level she's right—that we can't anticipate how much work Bubble is going to be until he gets here—but I don't admit that to her. *She* might have felt like she had to choose between raising a child and having a life of her own, but I refuse to think that's my only option.

I get her settled into my office as soon as I can. She glances around.

"What a cute little space you have here," she says. "Lots going on."

I've never been the sort of girl who kept a super clean, minimalist office. I've always been the girl with a hundred things tacked up on the walls, sticky notes everywhere, and piles of paper on every surface.

"You're just like your dad," my mom says. "He always had a messy office, too."

Something about her tone prickles at me. "It's not messy. I know where everything is."

"Oh, sweetheart," she says. "It's still messy, even if you think you can find things." She glances around again. "This is what happens when you don't have a woman around to teach you how to keep things tidy."

She says the last bit almost to herself, but whether or not she intends me to hear it doesn't matter.

"Well, maybe you should've thought of that before you left us," I say. "Good luck with your apartment search. I have things to do." I don't wait for her response. I spin around and march down the hall toward the classrooms.

Why didn't I listen to Calder and leave her at home? I ask myself. It's going to be a long day—my back already hurts, and my shoes are pinching my swollen feet. I can't deal with her little comments about my life.

But another part of me feels like I'm being too hard on her. *She just wants to make sure you're okay. She's trying to make up for the time she's lost.*

Well, that's another thing she should have thought of before she walked out the door.

I stop at the first classroom and rub my eyes. My headache has started early today, and I can already tell it's going to be a bad one—I'll be lucky if I make it to lunch without getting sick. I hate feeling like this—it's like my body has turned on itself. All I want to do is keep living my life, but Bubble insists on making things difficult.

Only a couple weeks more, I remind myself. *Then your son will be in your arms and all of this will be a memory.* Hopefully by then my mom will have her own apartment, too. Then things won't be quite so complicated. Reuniting with my mom was always going to be hard, no matter when or how it happened. I just need to stay strong. Be patient.

And come to a compromise with Calder. The last thing I want is to be constantly arguing in the last couple of weeks before our son's birth.

I glance through the window into the classroom beyond. Our summer art camps are currently in session, and this particular classroom houses our youngest group—some are hardly out of preschool.

What will you be like, Bubble? I think. *Will you take after your father?* In my mind I see a little boy with a mop of dark hair and those deep Cunningham eyes. Will he be as serious as Calder? Or will he be wild and silly like that little boy in the classroom who's currently trying to paint his own hair? Either way, I can't wait to meet him.

I take a deep breath, composing myself, and walk into the classroom.

I love my work—always have. And I didn't think it was possible, but I love it even more now that I run my own branch of the Frazer Center. I built this place—took my dad's dream and expanded it to fill my own. Over the next hour, I go from classroom to classroom, chatting with the teachers and students and overseeing the various projects. There's nothing like watching a child's face light up as she creates something with her bare hands.

I'm just leaving the final classroom when I hear a familiar voice coming down the hall.

"Good to see you too," I hear my dad say. "And you better call me about the game later."

The bottom drops out of my stomach. I love my dad, but he's the last person I want to see right now—especially with my mom just down the hall in my office.

He doesn't know about her return yet. I know I should have called him the moment she walked back into my life, but I didn't know quite how to break it to him. I didn't want to make an already awkward situation even more complicated. And then the days started ticking by and it felt like I'd waited *too* long.

My dad just got engaged to Regina, the woman he's been seeing for the last couple of years. The last thing he needs is my mom coming back and mucking things up. Because I have no doubt that she'll be just as tactless with him as she has been with me.

"Sweetheart," he says when he sees me, his face brightening. "You're glowing today."

He's just flattering me, I know. I can't remember

the last time I had a good night's sleep, and my head is still throbbing—but the ache has subsided to a slightly more manageable level. My back still hurts, though, and I try not to let it show as I waddle over to him.

"Hey, Dad," I say, praying that my mom doesn't hear us. I throw a glance over my shoulder toward my office, but so far the coast is clear. "I wasn't expecting a visit from you today."

"I know," he says, looking a little shamefaced. "I meant to call you, but I've been a little spacey recently. Regina has been running me ragged all week. She wants to get the caterer and the flowers and the music all settled by Friday, and there was some big mix-up with the invitations, and there's some drama with her second cousin or something. Now I understand why you kept your wedding so small." He rubs the back of his head. "Who'd have thought I'd be dealing with all of this again at my age? But my lady knows what she wants."

I smile. Regina has been a good thing for my dad—it's been a long time since I've seen him this happy. *All the more reason to get him out of here before he sees Mom.*

"How have you been, honey?" he asks.

"Just fine, Dad." We've reached the end of the hall, and I glance around, trying to decide where to lead him next.

"You're taking care of yourself, I hope. The little one is doing well?"

"Of course." I rub my belly. "He still likes to kick me at all hours of the night. He's a strong one, that's for sure."

"That's good." His smile spreads. "You were

pretty energetic at that stage yourself, I remember." He doesn't mention my mom—he never does, and I've always just pretended I don't notice.

I throw another glance down the hall. Dad needs to know what's going on, but not here and now, when she's only fifty feet away.

"Is there a particular reason you stopped by today?" I ask him.

His cheeks color a little. "Honestly, I just needed a little break. I don't mind helping with all the wedding stuff, you know, but after a while it all just starts to blur together. I decided to leave it to Regina for today and get a little change of scenery."

Normally I'd be happy for his company, but not today. *Why, why, why didn't I listen to Calder and leave her back at the estate?*

"Well, I'm sure Regina has it under control," I say. I need to figure out how to get him out of here without being rude. "Hey—do you mind running a couple of errands for me? There are some supplies we need and I'm swamped." I feel a twinge of guilt for lying to him, but I don't know how else to handle the situation gracefully. There's been enough drama around my mom already.

"Sure," he says. "Anything you need, honey. Should I grab us lunch later?"

"I—"

"Sweetheart, is that you I hear?" My mom's voice floats down the hall. "I need help with—" She stops dead still, her eyes widening when she sees my dad.

Dad looks just as stunned. His mouth has fallen open slightly and his bushy eyebrows twitch.

"David?" my mom says. "Is that you?"

"Michelle?" My dad's voice is strangely breathless.

He looks stunned. Confused.

And before I can make any explanations, the confusion in his eyes turns to anger. He spins towards me. "What is she doing here?"

"Oh, David," my mom says, stepping closer. "Don't get mad at her."

"I'm not mad at her," he snaps. "I'm merely wondering what you said to weasel your way back into her life."

I hold out my arms, trying to keep the two of them apart. "You guys, let's take this back into my office."

"Yes," my mom says. "Let's not cause a scene, David. This is our daughter's place of work."

"I know that," my dad says. "I know that much better than you, in fact. I helped her open this place. What have you been doing all this time? Gallivanting with some used-car salesman and getting your nails done?"

It's strange to see my dad so angry. He rarely loses his temper. I've never heard him speak with such venom in his voice, and I've definitely never seen the look he has in his eyes right now.

"David," my mom says. "It wasn't like that. You know it wasn't like that. I tried to tell you—"

"So now it's my fault? You left because I wasn't a good listener?"

"Guys," I say again. "Please, let's discuss this somewhere a little more private."

"I'm not the one making this difficult," my mom says, but she turns and walks back down the hall toward my office.

My dad is fuming beside me. His ears are bright red, and the twitch in his eyebrow has grown violent.

"How long have you been in contact with her?" he

asks me. His voice is strangely quiet.

"She showed up at the estate about a week and a half ago," I tell him. "She said she had nowhere else to go. I didn't know what to do."

"You should have told me," he says. His jaw is rigid, and I can tell he's trying very hard not to turn his anger on me, but he's having trouble. "You should have called."

"I know." And now it's coming back to bite me in the ass. He shouldn't have had to find out this way. "But I was trying to understand… I didn't know what I was feeling. I was just trying to make sense of it all, and I knew you'd be upset, and—"

"Damn right I'm upset! That woman had no right to—" He lets out a sigh, and when he speaks again he's managed to calm himself. "I'm sorry, sweetheart. This is just a lot to handle." He tilts his head slightly, looking me over. "How are you doing? Are you all right?"

"I'm okay," I say, letting my hand drift across my stomach. Bubble is moving again. He doesn't like people fighting. "I'm just confused. And trying to do the right thing." *And my head is throbbing again, and my back hurts, and I just want to lie down and nap until this all goes away.*

My dad lets out another sigh. "I suppose we should go talk to her, then."

We follow her down the hall. I don't know what I'm going to do. I knew this inevitable meeting was going to be awkward, but I never expected it to escalate so quickly. For all that I've been trying to deal with this on my own, I desperately wish Calder were here to help me handle these two. I might not agree with him about what to do, but I know he'd get it done.

When we reach my office, I pull the door closed behind us. It's probably better if we aren't interrupted.

"Are you both prepared to talk about this like adults?" I say.

That earns me glares from both of them, but I just cross my arms. They might be my parents, but they're the ones who just got into a fight out in the hall.

"I'm fine," my mom says. "It's David you should worry about."

My dad starts to rise out of his chair. "Now, just you wait—"

"Guys," I say. "No provoking each other." I smooth my hand across my belly, trying to pacify Bubble. *God, my whole body aches.* "Look, I owe both of you an apology. Dad, I should have told you that Mom was back. And Mom, we should have had a discussion about Dad. I didn't know he was coming in today, but I should've made it clear that he's still a big part of my life and that there was a chance we would be seeing him. Now, let's start over."

For a moment, the two of them just glare at each other. But at least they aren't shouting—something for which my throbbing skull is eternally grateful.

Finally, my mom straightens and folds her manicured hands in her lap.

"I'm sorry, David," she says. "I should have contacted you myself. You were never very good at dealing with surprises."

My dad's lips press into a hard line. "This has nothing to do with how well I deal with surprises," he says, and though his voice is calm I can tell it's taking all of his effort. "It has everything to do with the fact that you think it's okay to just waltz back into our lives on a whim."

"I know I hurt you, David. But I don't think—"

"It's not me I'm concerned with," he says. "It's our daughter."

"And I'm trying to make up for that," my mom says. "I love her. I want to make this right. And believe it or not, I still love you—"

"Don't give me that shit," my dad says, actually rising out of his chair this time. "If you loved us, you wouldn't have walked away like you did. You wouldn't have gone twenty years without sending word to either of us. This is not about loving us or doing the right thing. This is about easing your conscience, nothing more." He sighs and sinks back down. "You've always been flighty, Michelle. I should have seen it coming. But I wanted to believe the best in you."

My mother's back is straight, her hands still carefully folded. She raises her chin slightly. "Well, you weren't exactly a saint, either."

"Let's try to keep this civil," I say. I sit on the edge of my desk and try to keep my breathing steady. Bubble keeps jabbing me with his foot, and he's strong enough these days that it actually kind of hurts. "Yes, this is awkward. Yes, this is confusing and emotional. But we have time to figure it out. We don't have to sort out all of our feelings today."

My dad looks sharply at me. "What do you mean by that? You intend to let her be a part of your life?"

"I'm looking to move to Barberville," my mom says. "I plan to stay here for a while."

"I don't believe a word you say about your intentions," my dad says. "You told me you loved me and wanted to spend the rest of your life with me. You told me you wanted half a dozen kids. You told me a lot of things, Michelle, and most of them turned out to be lies."

"Really, David—just because our marriage didn't work out doesn't mean I'm lying now."

"Forgive me if I think that's a load of crap."

"Guys," I say. "Maybe it's better if we just leave this for now. Give this a chance to sink in and let everyone have a little time to think this through." *Is it just me, or did it suddenly get unbearably warm in this room?* My head is pounding so hard I can hardly think straight, and Bubble refuses to sit still. *I know*, I think to him. *I don't like this, either.* The pain in my lower back is spreading, and all of this just feels like too much work. I'm so tired, so achy, so... depleted.

"All the time in the world won't change my mind on this," my dad is saying. He looks over at me. "I know she's your mom, sweetheart, and I know you're an adult, but I suggest you think long and hard about the decision to let her back into your life. This woman is a master of emotional manipulation."

For the first time, some emotion flickers across my mom's face. "I am not emotionally manipulating her, David. I resent that accusation." Her gaze turns to me. "If anyone is an emotional manipulator here, honey, it's your dad. I spent so long—"

"Don't you dare call her *honey*," Dad says. "You lost the right to treat her like your daughter when you walked out the door."

Shut up! I want to scream. *Both of you, just shut up!* Bubble throws another punch at my ribs, and I grit my teeth as I grip the edge of the desk. Between the headache and the lower back pain I'm starting to feel nauseated again. I think I might be sick right here in the middle of my office.

Calder, I wish you were here... He would make all of this go away.

Meanwhile, my parents keep going at it.

"How dare you—"

"If you think—"

"The nerve of you—"

"Do you have any idea—"

The nausea rises in my chest, and I reach for the cup of water on my desk. There's a tightening in my abdomen, an ache that's growing more insistent by the second.

"Hush," I whisper to Bubble. "It's all right, little one. It's all right."

But all the soothing words in the world can't stop the wave of angry, resentful energy coming from the two people in front of me.

"I spent so many years—"

"I can't believe that you—"

"I'm disgusted—"

"How can you even think that—"

The pain in my lower body is growing sharper, tightening almost unbearably. My hand begins to shake, and I set the water back down before I spill it everywhere.

"You guys," I say, but my shaking voice is lost beneath the arguing.

"If you knew what—"

"Me? Why don't you—"

"You guys." *This can't be happening. Not here. Not yet.* I try to hold onto the desk for support, but I only end up knocking my water to the floor. The cup crashes against the linoleum.

Both of my parents instantly go silent. They turn to me, and I can tell by the way both of their faces suddenly change that I must look as bad as I feel.

"Guys, I—" Suddenly, everything seems to be closing in on me. My ears are ringing. My heart is beating too fast. I feel like I can't breathe. Panic has taken over.

Both of them leap toward me at once.

"Honey."

"Sweetheart."

Their hands are on me, but I don't have the presence of mind to tell which hand belongs to which parent. I don't have the presence of mind for anything at all. My panic is getting worse, cutting off my air and making my heart gallop faster and faster.

And as the fear settles in, all I can think of over and over again is, *I need Calder.*

10
CALDER

That was too close.

My jaw hurts from clenching. My mind won't slow down. I've been pacing the same spot on the floor for so long that I'm surprised I haven't worn a hole into the boards.

It was only a false alarm, I remind myself. Lily is fine—for now—and the doctor said she was only having Braxton Hicks contractions, probably made worse by stress. But even though she's now safe in our bed, I still can't seem to make myself calm down. When it comes time for the real thing… I don't even want to think about it.

"There's no need to be so worked up," Lily tells me. "Everything is fine. Come to bed."

"Everything is not all right," I say. "Your mother upset you so much that you—"

"It was my dad's fault, too," she says. "And it was

a false alarm. I'm all right. No harm done."

"Maybe not this time, but I'm not willing to take that chance again." I resume my pacing. "That woman needs to go."

"I agree," she says. "And she's already looking for a place. But in the meantime, she has nowhere else to go and—"

"There are a hundred places she could go," I say. "She's managed to survive without you for most of her life. She's a resourceful woman. I'm sure she can figure something out."

Lily takes a deep breath. "I know you're a little upset—"

"A little? Lily, that woman—"

"—but it's too late to do anything about it tonight."

I stop pacing and look down at her. She looks so soft, so frail right now—and so vulnerable. Beneath the exhaustion in her eyes is something unspeakably tender and afraid.

"We need to figure something out," I say, gently but firmly. "I can't do this, Lily. I can't watch her do this to you."

"It was a difficult pregnancy even before she showed up," Lily says. "There was always a high chance of me ending up on bed rest, even without her around."

"But that woman isn't helping. I don't want you to have any stressors, anything that upsets you in even the slightest way."

She closes her eyes. "I'd be upset if we kicked her out. I'd be worried about her."

The same way she worried about you all these years? I want to ask her. *You were a child when she left, but that didn't stop her from thinking only about herself.* But I don't say it. I don't need to remind her of the truth. She knows the truth, but she's stubbornly ignoring it anyway.

"I don't want to argue anymore," she says softly, opening her eyes and reaching her hand out to me. "Come to bed."

I move closer to the bed and clasp her fingers in mine. "I'm afraid I'm too worked up to go to bed."

"I can work with that," she says. She lifts my hand to her lips and kisses the inside of my palm. Her tongue licks against my skin.

At the first touch, desire rushes through me. It would be easy to sink down onto the bed and take her, to distract myself from my thoughts in the pleasure of her body. But that wouldn't be right.

"I think we should take a break tonight," I say, and though I don't take my hand completely out of her grip, I still pull it away from her soft mouth.

"Are you sure about that?" she says in that sweet, innocent tone that gets me every time. The look she's giving me doesn't help, either. "I could use a little release right now."

Me too, I think. But things have changed. "You're on bed rest. That means you need to rest." It takes all of my effort to say those words.

"I don't want to rest. I just want to be in your arms."

And God, that's where I want her, too. I want to devour her, to spare no part of her skin from my lips. I want to assure myself that every inch of her is all right. That she's well and whole and healthy. That her heart still beats as it should and our son still moves inside of her. It doesn't matter what she says—I can't look at her without seeing the risk. She's everything to me. *Everything.* And having her now feels too dangerous—no less because I know she's trying to distract me from the real issue again.

"Seduction won't work on me tonight," I say, pulling out of her grip. "We need to figure out what we're going to do about your mother."

She doesn't say anything, but I see the emotions flicker across her face—surprise, anger, fear, hurt. I don't think I've ever rejected her advances before, but I know I can't tell her the truth—that my cock is already half hard, that it's taking all of my power not to pull her into my arms—without losing my resolve.

And then, just when I think the look on her face can't make me feel any worse, her eyes start to glisten with tears. She squeezes them shut and leans back against her pillow, shaking her head from side to side. Her chest rises and falls with a shuddering breath and her hands grip the comforter.

"I don't know what to do," she says in a rough whisper. "Please, please let's not talk about this tonight. Please."

Hearing her beg me like that makes my chest ache. *God, what have I done?* A tear leaks from beneath her dark lashes, and it nearly breaks me. I can't bear to see her cry. I can't bear to see her in any sort of pain, and I hate that I've done something that made her suffer, even in a small way.

"I'm just so tired," she says, pressing her hands against her eyes. "I'm so tired. And I don't know what to do, and I'm confused, and I'm... afraid."

I sit down on the edge of the bed and take her hand. "Lily, I won't let anything happen to you." I'd die before I let any harm come to her. Throw down my life in a heartbeat if I thought it would ease her pain.

"I know," she says, her eyes still closed. "I know, I just… God, I'm so tired."

It's torture, hearing her voice crack like that. Seeing the anxiety in her face. And I'm sitting here like a damned helpless fool, unable to do a single fucking thing.

"Get some sleep," I tell her. "I don't want you thinking or worrying about anything else." I slide my hand across her cheek, even though I know she's beyond the place where a gentle touch will give her much comfort. *Damn this… damn it straight to hell.* Watching her struggle, knowing I can't take this pain from her, is the worst kind of agony.

"Lie down next to me," she whispers. "I promise I won't try to… I just need you to hold me. Just be with me." Her eyes finally open, and she looks at me with a need that has nothing to do with physical lust.

She doesn't need to ask me twice. Quickly, I undress and turn down the lights, then slide into bed next to her. She falls into my arms with a shuddering sigh, and I wrap myself around her, holding her against me.

"I'm not going to let anything happen to you," I tell her again, my fingers grazing her spine.

"I know," she whispers against my skin. "I… I just…"

The Lily I know is so strong, so stubborn, that hearing her fall apart torments me in a way I don't know how to bear. It isn't enough to just hold her. That's my son she has growing inside of her, and I need to fix this somehow.

"If there's anything you need, just say the word," I

tell her. "I don't want you focused on anything but taking care of yourself and our son. I'll manage everything else."

She stiffens. "Just promise me you won't send my mom away."

I can't promise her that, not when her mother is a major part of the problem. But even though I don't say that out loud, she knows how to read my silence.

"Promise me, Calder," she says.

"Why do you insist on allowing her to disrupt your life?" I say. "Lily, there will be plenty of time to connect with her after our son is here."

"But she's here now. She needs our help now."

"She's an intelligent, capable woman. She'll manage for a few weeks just fine, I'm sure." I press my lips against her hair. "Lily, think of your health. Think of our son's health. Your mother will still be there after all of this is over."

Her grip tightens on me. "But what if she isn't?"

The way she says this—the way her voice breaks on the final word—makes me realize we've hit on the core of her fears.

"You think she might leave you again," I say carefully.

She presses her face into my shoulder. "I... I don't know. I don't know what I think." She lets out a long, shaky breath. "I want to believe that she's really had a change of heart. I want to believe it so, so badly. And if that's true, if she's honestly ready to be a part of my life again... then how can I turn her away? Maybe there's a reason the universe sent her back into my life now, when I'm about to have a baby. Maybe she and I need each other." She squeezes me. "But I'm also afraid that... I'm afraid if I let her in, if I find a way to get past all of my anger, she'll just..."

"She'll hurt you again," I finish for her.

She nods against my shoulder. "I guess I've just been waiting for her to ask us for money, or to... to... I don't know what. I don't know what I think about any of this, and that's the problem. It's the not knowing that makes it so hard." Her lashes tickle my skin. "I know you think I'm crazy, that I'm being blinded by my emotions, but I can't help it. It doesn't matter how angry I am or how much she annoys me—I still want her to want me." She whispers this last part. "I just want her to want me."

I rest my chin on the top of her head, holding her as close as I can, given the roundness of her belly. She's quivering beneath my hands, and it's clear that this is all too much.

"Just sleep," I tell her. "We don't need to decide anything tonight."

She shifts in my arms. "Promise me you won't send her away."

"You know I can't do that, Lily."

She starts to sit up, but I grab her arms.

"I promise that I will only act in your best interest," I tell her. "But so help me, Lily, if I think it's in your best interest to get that woman out of our home, nothing will stop me. Not even you."

She jerks out of my grip. "I would never, *ever* force you to turn your back on your family."

"Even if my health depended on it? Even if our child's life depended on it?" I sit up beside her.

Fury flashes in her eyes. "Are you *still* trying to accuse me of not caring about our son's life?"

"No. I'm saying that your life and our son's life mean more to me than your mother's feelings. And I refuse to promise you that I'll put her needs above yours."

"That's not what I was asking."

"It might as well have been."

"This is ridiculous," she says, starting to get out of the bed.

I grab her arms again. *God, where did this go wrong?* I'm supposed to be calming her, not making her even more upset.

"Please, Lily, just lie down. Get some sleep. You've had a really long day."

For a moment, I think she's going to fight me, but then she squeezes her eyes shut and all of the energy seems to leave her. Half a dozen emotions war on her face as she sinks back down onto the pillows.

Now just try to get her to sleep without putting your foot in your mouth again. I stand by everything I've said tonight, but I won't push it. Not now.

"We'll figure out everything tomorrow," I tell her softly, pulling her toward me again. "Just get some rest."

She twists so that her back is nestled against my chest. She's still angry with me—I can tell by the stiffness of her body—but she doesn't say anything.

I wait until her breathing has slowed, until her muscles begin to relax. And then I slide my hand slowly across her belly. Through her nightdress, beneath my palm, I feel a little push as our son moves inside of her. My chest tightens.

This is what I live for, this life in my arms, I think. I remember feeling my sister's stomach when she was pregnant, being amazed by the life growing inside of her. But now that it's my wife, my son… it's nothing short of miraculous.

"I love you," I murmur to her. "I love you so much, Lily."

I can't tell if she's still awake. But either way, she doesn't answer.

11
LOU

I'm in the office on the south side of the house, working out some of the final details of my surprise honeymoon trip for Ward, when Calder stalks into the room.

"Good morning," I say—though you'd hardly know it was morning, considering how overcast it is outside today. When I glance up and see his face, my fingers freeze on the computer keyboard. "What's wrong? Is it Lily?"

We had a bit of a scare yesterday, what with Lily getting rushed to the hospital. She'll be on bed rest for the duration of her term, but both mother and baby are healthy—or so I thought. Calder looks like he's hardly slept. There are dark circles under his eyes, and he seems agitated.

"We need to figure out what Lily's mother wants," Calder says, jerking a hand through his hair. "It's that woman's fault that Lily is in this state."

I lean back in my chair and glance over at Ramona. She's in her playpen over by the window, and she's pulled herself up onto her feet so that she can watch her uncle with wide, curious eyes.

"What does Lily think about this?" I ask him.

"She's confused," he says as he starts to pace in front of the desk where I'm sitting. "She's upset, but she doesn't want to hurt her mother. She feels guilty about the whole thing. She—" He stops suddenly and rubs the side of his face. "She still has emotional ties to the woman. I understand that. But if her mother is using her, or if she's just going to hurt her again, then I'm not going to stand by and let that happen."

Calder has never been the sort of guy to admit he might be wrong, or to stop fighting for his own way—but in this case, I think he might have a point. It would be all too easy for someone to take advantage of Lily right now. And I can't exactly say I like our guest—tensions have definitely been high in this house since she showed up, and it's clearly putting a strain on Calder and Lily's relationship.

"Did you sleep at all last night?" I ask him.

He gives a jerk of his head and resumes pacing. "No. I can't let this go on."

"How's Lily?"

"She's still sleeping, thank God. She's exhausted herself trying to handle all of this." His fingers are in his hair again. "I've never seen her like this before. She's going to kill herself with stress, Louisa. And I can't watch her do it. I can't." He stops once more, spinning toward me. "What do you think I should do?"

He's stopped right in front of Ramona's playpen.

Though he doesn't seem to notice her, she smiles at him—she's got her dad's grin—and reaches up with a squeal.

I shift my attention back to my brother. "I think you should do what's best for the both of you. But don't assume that you're the only one who knows what that is. Lily is a smart woman, even if she is dealing with a bunch of emotional crap right now, and her opinion matters, too."

He shoots me a look that tells me that wasn't the answer he wanted. Beside him, Ramona starts babbling, and he finally looks down at her, his face softening slightly.

"That doesn't really help me," he says, looking defeated. Forget Lily—it's my brother who's going to let stress drive him to an early grave.

"I never claimed I was an expert at giving sibling advice," I tell him. "If you don't like what I have to say, you can always ask Ward."

He raises an eyebrow as if to say, *Are you kidding me?* before looking back down at Ramona. I love both Ward and my brother, but those two can be such big, stubborn idiots when it comes to each other. It's like suggesting to either of them that they might learn something from the other undermines their manliness or something. *Men.*

Calder bends over slightly, offering his finger to the grasping Ramona. My daughter squeals in delight, her curls bobbing as she grabs it.

But though my brother smiles at Ramona, he's still too rigid.

"What exactly are you so worried about?" I ask him. "Lily's on bed rest now. You can keep her mom away from her pretty easily."

"It's not just that," he says, straightening. "It's more than just the fact that she upsets Lily." Ramona whimpers and pouts when he pulls his hand away from her, then looks at me with those big eyes as if to say, *Mom! Make my uncle play with me!*

But Calder is distracted again, and he clasps his hands behind his back as he starts pacing once more.

"What else is it?" I ask.

"I don't trust that woman's motives," he says. "I don't think she's here for the right reasons. Lily doesn't trust her either, but I think she's afraid to press the matter."

I consider this. "You think she wants money."

"Yes, that's exactly what I think."

"Has she asked for it yet?"

"No. But that doesn't mean she won't."

I prop my hands behind my head. "The way I see it, there's one simple way to figure that out once and for all."

"Which is?"

"To offer her money. See how much it takes for her to agree to leave."

"You mean I should try to pay her off."

I can tell by his tone that he's already been considering this option, but I suspect he's trying to gauge whether bribing her is a step too far.

"You don't actually have to pay her off," I tell him. "Just offer it and see how she reacts. You'll have your answer right there. Of course, if you take that route and her intentions have been good all along, you risk driving her away. And pissing off your pregnant wife, which is never a good thing. But you'll have your answer, at least."

Calder heaves a sigh. "I know. Seeing Lily like

this... It's worth every risk for me. I can bear her anger. I can't bear her pain." Though he looks away from me, I've already seen the shadows in his eyes. This pregnancy has really done a number on him.

"It sounds a little evil, offering her a bribe," I say carefully. "But if it sets your mind at ease, then maybe it's worth it."

"All Lily really needs is an answer," he says. "She needs to know once and for all whether she can trust this woman."

"And if her mom really wants the best for her, maybe she'll see that we're only trying to protect her."

Calder nods and gives his already disheveled hair one more sweep with his hand. "God, I hope so."

"You'll get through this," I say. "Both of you. Lily is strong. She can handle a lot more than you think."

"I don't want her to have to handle anything." Still, now that he's made his decision, he seems to have calmed a little.

"Well, that's not exactly how life works," I tell him. "Now pick up Ramona before she starts crying. She's going to throw a tantrum if you don't pay her some attention."

He looks back over at his niece, and this time the hint of a genuine smile creeps across his lips. "All right."

He strides over to her playpen and bends over, picking her up into his arms. Ramona grins and cries, "Puh puh puh!" as he gets her settled.

"What does that mean?" he asks me.

I smile and shrug. "You'll have to ask her."

For a moment, he just holds her, bouncing her slightly as she babbles and grabs at his shirt. He's almost smiling at her, but I suspect from the glint in his eye that he's not really here—that instead he's thinking about his own kid.

You have no idea what you're getting into, Big Brother, I think. If he's this agitated and distressed before the baby even gets here, then he's in for a big surprise when he actually has a living, breathing human depending on him. The pregnancy is just the warm-up round.

"Oh," he says suddenly, bringing me out of my thoughts. "I meant to tell you. I've made those inquiries about Taran Harker."

I sit up straighter. "Have you heard anything?"

He shakes his head. "Not yet. But these things take time. And there's always the chance that he doesn't want to be found." He pulls his collar out of Ramona's hand. "I'll make sure to update you if I get any news."

"Thanks." I lean back in my chair. I'm still not sure how I feel about finding our alleged half-brother, but it looks like I don't have to decide that yet.

We are going to be all right, I think. *All of us.* Just as long as my brother doesn't do anything stupid.

12
CALDER

It's two days before I can get Lily's mother alone.

Two days of trying to keep that woman from upsetting my wife even more. Two days of tension between Lily and me. Two days of Lily trying to convince herself that everything will be okay.

I finally corner the woman out in the garden. The sky is rather gray today—the weather's been dreary all week—and there's an unseasonable chill in the air. A cold front is moving in, and the news reports are predicting quite a storm tonight. For now, though, the sky is dry.

For a moment, I just watch Lily's mother from afar, trying to read her. She's been quiet since Lily's incident, and I can't tell whether that's a good or a bad sign.

After a couple of minutes, she looks up and sees me.

"Why, good afternoon, Calder," she says. She gives me a smile I've seen before, one that doesn't quite reach her eyes. Everything about this woman seems disingenuous—the too-red hair, the fake nails, the bright makeup. I don't like it. "What brings you out here?"

"There's something I wish to speak with you about," I say.

"Is it Lily?" To her credit, she seems genuinely concerned. But just because some part of her still cares for her daughter doesn't mean that she doesn't want anything from us. I frown as I cross the distance between us. I thought I knew exactly what I wanted to say to this woman, but now that I'm here, now that I finally have her alone, I'm having trouble finding the words.

This woman is Lily's mother. Sometimes, at the right angle, I can see it—something in her eyes, in the shape of her cheekbones, in the set of her shoulders. Once or twice I've even heard it in her voice. There are pieces of Lily in this woman. Whether I like it or not, they share something. I've made plenty of ultimatums and driven many a hard bargain in my life, but this feels infinitely more personal. It almost makes me second-guess my plan.

But then I think about Lily upstairs in our bed and how fragile and exhausted she looked this morning. This is all for her.

I stop a few feet in front of her. "Why are you here?"

She gives a dismissive laugh, and her beaded bracelets rattle as she flicks her wrist. "Why does everyone keep asking me that?"

"Because it's still not clear to anyone," I say. "I

think it's a fair question. Why did you suddenly decide to return to Lily's life? Why now?"

"I've told you that already," she says. "And Lily. I've just come out of a bad relationship, and I didn't have anywhere else to go."

"And what exactly are you looking for here?" I ask. "What do you want from us? What do you want from Lily?"

She almost looks offended. "I want what any mother wants—I want to spend time with my child."

I refuse to let her brush off my questions the way she's brushed off Lily's. "You didn't want to spend time with her twenty years ago. You've taken your time reviving your motherly instincts."

"I'll be the first to admit that I've made some mistakes," she says. "But that doesn't mean that I don't love my daughter. I just want to make things right again." She looks at me, and for a split second, I think I see true emotion in her eyes. "But you wouldn't understand. You're not trying to understand."

Do I have it wrong? As Louisa pointed out, there's only one way to learn the truth once and for all. "How much do you want?"

She blinks. For a moment, I see Lily in her again.

"What do you mean?" she asks.

"I think I'm being quite clear," I say. "How much money do you want? How much will it take to get you out of our lives?"

Her lips part. "Is that what you think I want? Money?"

"Isn't it?" I don't let her escape my gaze. "Can you honestly tell me you don't want any financial assistance from us? That you just happened to show up after all this time only a handful of months after your daughter moved into a mansion?"

"It's not like that," she says, her eyes drifting away from me. She suddenly seems less sure of herself. "I'll admit I was hoping for a little help... but..."

"Then what's your number?" I press. "I'm afraid I'm not a billionaire anymore. We don't have millions of dollars to throw your way. But I'll do what I can if you agree to walk away before you hurt Lily again. So what will it be—five thousand? Ten?"

"I..." For once, this woman seems to be at a loss for words.

I guess I hit the nail on the head. Part of me feels validated, but the rest of me is just disgusted.

"I can't do this on my own," she says.

"Tell me your price," I say. There's no need to drag this out. I'd give anything to protect Lily. Trade my soul to the Devil himself if it would get her and our son safely through this pregnancy. "I can write you a check this very moment." The sooner she's gone, the better.

There's something strange in her eyes now, but I can't tell if it's shame or surprise. *Did she really expect us to believe that she was only here to make nice?* But whatever emotions she's experiencing, she hides them again quickly. She presses her bright red lips together as she straightens her shoulders.

"Do you really think you can buy me off?" she says. "That you can pay me to stay away from my daughter?"

"Yes, I do."

I don't think she expected me to call her bluff. She looks around before meeting my gaze again.

"This isn't what I wanted," she says, and the words

tumble over each other. "I really did want to reconnect with Lily."

"If that's what you want, then you have time to do it after the baby gets here. In the meantime, you have a choice. I won't have you causing stress for her any longer."

"You act like it's my fault she's stuck in bed," she says.

"Isn't it? What did you think would happen when you walked back into her life? You don't get over something like your mother abandoning you. And it certainly doesn't help that you seem to have no problem commenting on every aspect of her life—on me, on her job, on the choices she and I have made together."

"I'm her mother. I just want to make sure she's safe and happy. That's my job."

"You quit that job long ago. And you're a fool if you don't think that left a scar on her." I've seen it in Lily's eyes every day since this woman walked into our lives, felt it beneath my hands as I've held her. I'm going to heal that scar, even if it takes me the rest of my life to do so—but first I have to deal with the problem causing the wound at the heart of it all.

"You don't understand what I've been through," she says softly. "Leaving her was the hardest choice I've ever made in my life. I know that from the outside it looked like a selfish decision, but if I'd stayed there, I would have been miserable. I never would have been the mother she needed me to be, and I would have only come to resent her. Better for her to have no mother at all than to experience that."

"All I know is that nothing would ever induce me to leave my child," I say, thinking of the miracle I've felt moving inside of Lily. "Nothing. When you bring a child into the world, they are your responsibility. You get over yourself and do what's best for them. And that's what I'm asking you to do now."

"So leaving her when she was younger was a crime, but leaving her now is a gift?" She gives a bitter laugh. "Do you even hear yourself?"

"I'm asking you one more time," I say. "What is your price?"

"I can't believe this is happening," she says, but the indecision is clear on her face.

"This is your final chance," I tell her. "Tell me what you want and leave, or I swear, you'll never see a penny out of us."

She's silent for a long moment, and then she turns her face away from me. I wait patiently, and I suspect she's going over the numbers in her head, trying to guess how high I'm willing to go.

When she looks back at me, her eyes are shining with tears. She raises a hand to her cheek and flicks one of the drops away before speaking.

"It's been clear to me from the moment we met that you love her very deeply," she says. "So I guess I shouldn't be surprised that it's come to this."

I have to admit, I'm a bit taken aback by her words. "Excuse me?"

"You'd do anything for her. I see that." She gives a sad smile. "No one has ever loved me like that. In fact, I was beginning to think that sort of love didn't even exist. I can't say I agree with how you're handling things, but I also can't say that I don't understand." She pauses, letting out a long breath. "Yes, I was going to ask you two for money. But not until after the baby was here. And not for the reasons you think." Her eyes rise to mine again. "I'm sick."

To say I'm surprised by her little speech is an understatement. But now I'm struggling to keep up. "Sick?"

She nods. "Cancer. My doctor says I might have a year—and that's being optimistic. He says my chances are slightly better if I opt for surgery and chemo, but I think I'd rather spend the last year of my life enjoying myself rather than suffering through one treatment after another."

I'm still trying to wrap my head around this. "So that story about your boyfriend stealing your money was a lie?"

She shrugs. "Part of that story is true. I was with someone, and he wasn't a very nice man by the end of things. I knew he was stealing from me, but I just couldn't bring myself to care, not after I found out about the cancer." She spreads her hands. "He wouldn't have stuck by me through my treatment. And I decided I had better things to do with the rest of my life."

Like trying to reconnect with her daughter.

This changes everything. Or at least, it changes how I feel about this woman and her motives. But if this is the truth, then why the hell didn't she just tell us so from the beginning?

She seems to read my thoughts. "I know this is a lot to dump on someone at once, especially after I've been gone for so long. That's why I didn't say anything to Lily. I didn't want to worry her. I know I don't deserve it, but I wanted to spend a little bit of time with her before…"

I rub the side of my nose. *How the hell do I deal with this?* I knew what to do when I thought this woman was trying to take advantage of us, but now I have an entirely new crisis on my hands.

What would Lily want? I ask myself. That's easy—even though it would upset her, she'd want to know the truth. But the thought of Lily losing her mother so quickly, from something like this... It makes my heart ache for her. This is the last thing she needs.

Still, I want to do the right thing by my wife. Knowing the truth would put her heart at ease, at least.

"We need to tell Lily," I say.

But Michelle—somehow, suddenly, she's not just *that woman* anymore—shakes her head. "She'll just want me to get the treatment. She'll make me fight it."

"Of course she will." Because Lily has the biggest heart of anyone I know. Because she'll fight for the life of anyone, even someone who's hurt her deeply.

Michelle doesn't seem particularly thrilled by my response. "Even if I wanted to fight it, I couldn't. I don't have the money, and my insurance only covers part of the treatment."

"We can help you." We'll figure it out somehow, I'm sure. I'll be damned if I let Lily suffer through the death of her mother, not if I can prevent it. "But first we need to tell Lily everything."

Michelle only shakes her head again. "Not until after the baby is here. She has enough to worry about."

I want to argue with her, but damn her, she's right.

"And one more thing," she says. "Maybe you were right about getting out of your hair for the time being—it might be best if I go stay at a hotel in Barberville for a little while."

Now that I know the truth, so many things are starting to make sense—the way she avoided talking about her life, the way she poked and prodded into Lily's choices, even the way she tried to pick up her relationship with Lily right where they'd left off—and I'm starting to believe that I misjudged her after all. But even though I understand why Michelle has been behaving the way she has, I still believe that it will be in Lily's best interest to deal with all of this after our son has arrived.

"I can take you into town," I say.

She folds her hands in front of her, and I find myself looking for traces of Lily in her face.

"I might have to borrow some money," she says, looking a little embarrassed. "I have a little tucked away in a secret account, but not enough for a couple of weeks at a hotel."

"I'll get you whatever you need," I say.

One way or another, I'm going to do what's right for this family. Give Lily the peace of mind she needs as she enters the final phase of her pregnancy.

As for what we'll do after the baby is here—well, we'll figure that out when the time comes.

* * *

Less than two hours later, Michelle and I are in Barberville and I've got her set up at a modest little extended stay hotel just outside of downtown. I've prepaid for a two-week stay, and after that, I'll reassess the situation and figure out the best course of action. Michelle told Lily that she was looking for a job in the area, but since learning the truth about her health, I'm not sure whether that was an empty claim or not. Either way, though, now is not the time to be making any rash decisions. Lily comes first. We'll deal with Michelle after the baby is here.

I'm getting ready to leave when a thought occurs to me.

"Lily will have lots of questions when she learns the truth. And she'll want you to start treatment as soon as possible."

She starts to protest. "I still don't think I want treatment—"

"At the very least, will you go talk to a doctor here in town? Explore your options? I'll pay for your visit, of course."

She hesitates, then nods. "All right."

I turn to go, then pause again, pulling out my wallet.

"I know you said you had enough money to cover your food, but here's a credit card just in case," I say. "And for that doctor."

She hesitates again, and I wonder if I've offended her somehow. Finally, though, almost reluctantly, she reaches out and takes the card.

"Thank you," she says. As I turn once more, she adds, "Lily is lucky to have you."

I pause with my hand on the door. "I would do anything for her."

When I get outside, the rain has started. It's just a drizzle, but the dark clouds on the horizon suggest that this is only the beginning. I duck my head and run across the parking lot to my car.

I'm not looking forward to the conversation I'm going to have with Lily when I get home. She was asleep when Michelle and I left, and I decided it was better not to wake her. She would only have tried to keep us from leaving. I'm still not sure what I'm going to say to her—Michelle insists that she doesn't want to tell Lily the truth, not yet. And since it's her secret to tell, I'm inclined to respect her wishes. Still, I hate the idea of misleading Lily in any way—especially when, without the truth, there's no way Lily will understand that this was the best option.

The doubts only get worse as I get closer to home. I'm still trying to process everything I discovered today. It's a lot to handle at one time—learning that I misjudged Michelle, that she's dying, that there might not be anything we can do—and I confess that I was expecting our conversation to go in an entirely different direction. I'd considered Michelle to be a difficult, tactless woman, but after she told me the truth, she became so understanding and reasonable about the situation with Lily. It was almost easy to get her into town.

Too easy.

You're just overthinking things, I tell myself. The emotion on her face was genuine—I've seen what her fake expressions look like—and I don't doubt that she's truly sick. But something just isn't sitting right with me.

She didn't jump on the money, I remind myself. *If she was trying to take advantage of you, she would have just accepted your offer.*

Still, there's something more about this whole situation that's bothering me—but for the life of me, I can't put my finger on *what*. It's a dark feeling in my gut, a knot of warning. Maybe it's just that this news about Michelle's cancer is still so new, so unexpected. Or maybe I'm just having a hard time getting past my first impression of her. She's out of our house for the time being. That's a good thing.

So why do I feel like the sky is about to fall?

The rain is coming down harder now, pounding against my windshield. In the distance, I hear the first rumble of thunder. This storm is rolling in fast. I tighten my grip on the steering wheel and force myself to focus on the road.

Just when I'm nearing the wooded road up to the estate, however, my phone rings. I hit the button on my steering wheel to answer the call.

"Hello?"

"Yes, is this Mr. Cunningham?" comes a woman's voice through my speakers. "This is Penny from the credit card division of Barberville Regional Bank. We noticed some suspicious activity on your card and wished to verify it with you."

I nearly steer the car off the road.

"What kind of activity?" I demand. *Maybe this is just about the hotel. It's probably unusual for someone to book a two-week stay at a hotel in the town where he lives.*

"It's our policy to notify customers whenever we see charges over a certain threshold in a short period of time," Penny says. "I'm seeing a charge of eleven hundred and thirteen dollars and sixty-eight cents for the Barberville Extended Stay Deluxe. Is this charge correct?"

I let out a sigh of relief. "Yes."

"Okay," she says. "I've marked that charge as correct. Next I'm seeing a charge for seventeen hundred and ninety-two dollars and twenty-four cents for TransOceanic Airways."

I slam on my brakes. *Oh, God—she's running.*

That can't be right. I only left the hotel twenty minutes ago. Would Michelle really turn around the moment my back was turned and use my own credit card to run away again? After everything she told me?

This has to be a mistake.

For the life of me, though, I can't think of any other explanation.

"That's a fraudulent charge," I tell the woman on the phone. "Anything after the hotel is a fraudulent charge. Freeze the card."

I don't wait for her response. I hang up and immediately turn the car around.

It hasn't been that long, I tell myself. *She probably made that charge from the hotel.* Part of me is still hoping this is all a mistake, but my gut tells me otherwise. Now all I have to do is get back to the hotel before she leaves for the airport.

I'm driving too fast for these weather conditions, but I don't care—I need to find that woman. Now.

My car weaves through traffic, blowing through lights and earning me a number of angry honks. It's a miracle I make it to the hotel without killing myself. I leap out of the car, not even bothering to lock it behind me as I run into the lobby.

I don't wait for the elevator. I run up the steps two at a time to the fourth floor, and though I'm out of breath, I don't even pause for a second at the top. I rush down the hall and pound on her door.

"It's Calder!" I say. "Open up!"

There's no response.

"I mean it, Michelle. What's going on here?"

Again, there's no response—except for the woman in the room next door poking her head out and frowning at me.

I should have known she wouldn't answer. But the room is under *my* credit card, which means I should have no trouble getting another key.

I rush back down to the lobby and up to the front

desk. It's a different woman than the one who was here when we checked in, and she looks rather startled by my appearance. I know I must look deranged, but that's the least of my worries right now.

"I need another key to Room 417," I tell her.

She frowns, then types something into her computer. After a second, she says, "What was your name?"

"Calder Cunningham," I tell her. "The room is under my name."

She does a double-take when I say my name, looking at me a little more closely. My family's name is well-known in this area—and in most of the country, thanks to the tabloids—but I know I don't look like myself right now, soaked and desperate as I am.

"I need that key," I press.

She straightens, apparently remembering her job. "I'm sorry, Mr. Cunningham, but I'm afraid the woman in that room just checked out."

"What do you mean she checked out? She checked in less than an hour ago!"

The woman shakes her head. "I'm sorry, sir. She said something came up and she couldn't stay after all. I can make sure you aren't charged for the room, but there will still be a cancellation and cleaning fee—"

"I don't care about the fees!" I say. "Just tell me where she went."

Her frown deepens. "I'm sorry, Mr. Cunningham. Sir. She didn't say. And it's not our policy to ask—"

"Never mind," I tell her. This is just wasting time. I turn and stalk back toward the door.

"Um, Mr. Cunningham?" she calls after me. "She

did leave a note."

Then why the hell didn't you say so in the first place? I turn around and march back up to the desk, grabbing the envelope she holds out.

Inside, I find a note scrawled on hotel stationery:

Calder—

I know you're going to think I'm a coward, but trust me, it's better this way. I got to thinking after you left, and I believe it's best for all of us that I just leave now. There is no easy path going forward. All of my options end with the same result— with Lily getting hurt.

She would have insisted I get treatment. She would have given me all the money you had to try and make things better. But it comes down to this—I don't want to spend the last days of my life with my daughter watching me die. She should be focused on the new life that's coming, on your precious little child—not on death.

And, honestly, I'd rather spend my last few months having adventures in Europe, not enduring endless chemo treatments. I don't want to fight the cancer, and that would have been another point of contention between Lily and me. I don't want to argue with her, not about this.

I rest easy knowing that she has you—a man who would give her anything. Keep her safe. Bring her joy. And love her with your whole heart, the way I should have.

If I had my say, I'd prefer that you not tell her about the cancer. I'd rather have her anger than her sadness, as I trust that my mistakes will only make her a stronger, better mother than I ever was to her.

All the best,
Michelle

P.S. I apologize for the charges on your credit card, but I trust that they come out to far less than that check you intended to write me.

I stand there staring at the note for a long time after I finish. Rain drips from my hair onto the stationery.

I should have seen this coming. How the hell did I not see this coming?

She's right—I do think she took the coward's way out. If she wants to leave, then fine—but not without explaining things to Lily. Not without saying goodbye. This will crush Lily, whether or not she learns about the cancer. I'm not going to let that woman abandon her daughter a second time.

I glance at my watch. If Michelle booked an international flight, there's probably still time to catch her at the airport. If I hurry.

I shove the letter into my pocket and run out the door into the rain, sprinting all the way to my car. It's pouring even harder now, pounding on the roof of the car and obscuring everything through the windshield. I left my phone on the center console, and when I glance down at it, I see the flashing icon that indicates a missed call.

From Lily.

How the hell am I going to break this news to her?

But I know the answer to that—I'm not. At least not until I've found Michelle. Then I'm going to let *her* do the explaining.

I'm sorry, Lily, I think. *I promise I'm doing all of this for you.*

And then I crank on my car and go.

13
LOU

It might be storming outside, but I'm determined to make today a little brighter.

"I have a surprise for you," I tell Ward.

It took me half an hour to find him after I put Ramona down for her afternoon nap. Even though I've insisted that he take a break from his restoration projects, Ward has continued to work, and I find him retouching the paint in a bedroom in the eastern wing. He's currently perched on a ladder with a paintbrush in his hand.

When he grins down at me, I know he couldn't be happier to see me.

"What sort of surprise?" he asks, and his expression makes my heart skip a beat. He climbs down the ladder and stands in front of me.

I drink him in as he wipes the back of his hand across his forehead. His t-shirt has streaks of paint on it, and there's a new hole in his jeans, but somehow all of it works together to make him look irresistibly yummy. Something wells up inside of me as I admire him—and the way he's looking at me right now brings the blood rushing to my cheeks.

I pull the folded sheets of paper from behind my back.

"I know we said we didn't want to make a big fuss about the wedding," I say. "And that we decided we didn't need a honeymoon. But I've been thinking a lot recently, and… well, it's probably easiest if you just look." I shove the papers into his hand.

He pushes his auburn hair back as he looks down at the notes I've just handed him. He's still smiling, but his brow wrinkles in confusion.

"I'm not sure I understand," he says after a minute. "What is this?"

"It's an itinerary for a honeymoon. Of sorts." I'm suddenly a little nervous—maybe I should have talked to him before planning any of this. "I've mapped out a road trip that takes us across the country. Coast to coast. You've already seen the Atlantic Ocean, but I thought you might want to see the Pacific, too."

He looks down at the papers again, flipping through the pages I've handed him. I've given him maps, lists of sights along the way, even suggestions of where we should stay.

"I know we thought a trip would be too much trouble—but, well, maybe we just shouldn't think of it as a honeymoon," I rush on. "I mean, we'd probably have to bring Ramona with us anyway, since I'd feel bad about leaving her with Lily and Calder when they'll be having a newborn to deal with. But it could be fun. Our first big trip as a family. And we'd get to see the whole country, just like we planned once." He looks up at me, and in his eyes I can see quite vividly that he remembers the promises, spoken and unspoken, that we made to each other when we first ran away together. "That trip changed me, Ward, but we never got to finish it. Let's finish it now."

He's still just staring at me, and this silence is so out of character that I don't know what to do.

"Well?" I ask him softly. "Do you want to go?"

"Do I..." A huge grin spreads across his face. "Lou, this is amazing."

Before I can respond, he catches me up in his arms, pulling me close. The pages of my itinerary flutter to the ground as his kiss envelops me, dragging me under.

After a moment, I break away. "You really like it?"

"I love it," he says, nuzzling his nose against mine. "Lou, there's nothing I want more than to go on another adventure with you. And our daughter." He raises his hands to my face, and his thumbs brush against my cheeks. "That trip changed me, too."

I laugh in relief. "It's silly, but for a moment there I thought you were upset."

"Upset? How could I be upset? Lou, no one has ever given me something like this before. How could I not love it?"

"I know," I say, feeling foolish. "But we'd agreed not to make a big fuss about getting married. And you've been so focused on your projects recently that I thought you might be hesitant to leave them."

"Lou," he says, growing serious. "The only reason I agreed to not make a big deal about getting married is because that's what I thought you wanted. At the end of the day, all that matters to me is that you're my wife. I'll take any of the trappings—or none of them. Whatever you want. If you want a honeymoon, then I do, too. I want all of it." He kisses me passionately, then pulls away again. "As for the renovations…" He looks up at his ladder. "I know I've been a little focused recently. But God, they're just projects. I didn't mean to make you think…" He releases me and steps away, rubbing the back of his head. "This is all for you. For you and Ramona. I just want to make this place into the home you deserve."

"This is already our home," I tell him.

"I know, I just…" He shrugs as he tries to find the words. "I guess I always thought that when I met the woman I was going to spend the rest of my life with, I'd get to build her a house with my own two hands. Or at least buy her one with my own money." He shakes his head. "I'm not explaining this right. It's just that I look around this place and I don't feel like any of it is *mine*. Everything we have was just handed to me. I didn't earn any of this."

I cross my arms. "What about me? Did *I* earn any of this?"

"You grew up here," he says. "This place was yours long before you ever met me."

"But I didn't *earn* it," I point out. "It was my home because my parents owned it. And now it's our home because *your* father owned it. It's no different."

"It's a little different," he says. "If it was given to me, then it can be taken away. I'm supposed to be providing for you and Ramona—"

"Is that what this is about?" I ask with a laugh. "Some outdated idea about a man needing to provide for his wife?" I mean it as a joke, but the look he gives me is dead serious.

"I want to make this place ours," he says. "Build something for us with my own hands."

I step closer to him. "You *are* building something. We both are. Every day we're together, we're building a life for our family. And that's true no matter where we are. This house doesn't matter."

He takes me in his arms again, his deep blue eyes searching mine. "I just want to be the man you deserve. The dad Ramona deserves. I'm afraid I'll never live up to that job."

His words so closely echo my own fears that I almost laugh. Instead, I fold myself against his chest. "How do you think I feel? You're the one who goes around telling me that I'm perfect and that I'm some sort of angel. How am I supposed to live up to *that*?"

He threads his fingers in my hair and pulls my head back so that I'm looking up at him. "You *are* per—"

"Neither of us is perfect," I say, cutting him off. "In fact, I think I might have encouraged my brother to try and bribe his mother-in-law. I'm pretty sure that's not something an angel would do."

His eyebrows rise. "You did *what*?"

"I told him he should ask you for advice, but he didn't want to listen." I feel a smile creeping on. "So let's just drop all this talk about trying to live up to impossible standards for each other. I love you, Ward. You are everything I could ever want in a husband and everything Ramona could ever need in a dad." I press myself closer to him. "And I love that you're trying to make this place ours. That you care so much about building us a home. Don't think for a minute that I will ever take that for granted—but also know that my home will always be in your arms, wherever we may be."

He touches his forehead to mine.

"I love you," he whispers. "And I don't care what you say, or even what you do—you'll always be too good for me. But that just means I intend to spend the rest of my life trying to make this world the best that I can for you and Ramona."

He doesn't let me respond. Instead, he drops his mouth to mine, catching me in a kiss.

And I'm just as eager to lose myself in him. Moments alone are rare enough these days, and I plan to take full advantage of this one. I reach between us and tug up his t-shirt, running my hands over his bare stomach and through the trail of hair that leads down into his jeans. I feel him smile against my lips.

"I just put Ramona down for her nap," I say. "So we have a little time before—"

I don't even get to finish the sentence. He yanks me hard against him and attacks my mouth again.

My body responds instantly. I open my lips beneath him, letting him in, and my fingers undo his fly. He's already backing me against the wall, and it's not until I'm pressed up against it that I remember what he was doing before I walked in.

I tear my lips away from his. "The paint!"

Ward freezes. But it's too late—I can already feel the wet, sticky paint clinging to my arms.

For a moment, neither of us moves. Neither of us seems to know what to do. But then, at the very same moment, we both burst out laughing. If I was afraid of getting dirty, I never would have married Ward.

I'm still laughing as I pull his face back down toward mine. "I'll get you back later."

He's grinning. "No doubt you will."

And then his mouth is on mine again.

I lean into his kiss, letting my hands continue their explorations beneath his shirt. He seems to have a similar idea, and his fingers move beneath my blouse to slide up the bare skin of my sides. We've had to be a little more creative with our *alone time* since Ramona came along, but Ward and I have managed just fine— mostly because neither of us seems to care where or when or how we come together. We can't seem to keep our hands off of each other.

His tongue slips into my mouth, teasing and exploring, and I start to push his pants down his hips. I need him. Now.

But as I do, something pulls me out of the moment.

"Did you hear that?" I ask.

Ward's face is still so close to mine that I can feel his breath on my lips. "No. But Ramona will be fine for a few—"

"It wasn't Ramona." I tilt my head, listening. "I thought I heard…"

This time, the voice is a little louder, closer.

"Is that Lily?" Ward says.

"She's supposed to be in bed," I say. "I wonder where Calder is. He'd freak if he knew she was up and about."

As much as I hate being interrupted, I have a sense deep in my stomach that something isn't right. Ward seems to share my feelings, and he's already pulling his pants back up.

The next time Lily calls, her voice is even clearer. She's calling for Calder. I wonder why she didn't just try his cell—he always has it on him, and it's usually the fastest way to find someone in this giant house.

I smooth down my blouse and hurry to the door while Ward is still buttoning his fly.

"Lily?" I call as I head down the hall. "Is everything all right? Do you need something?" Ward and I both offered to help when she was put on bed rest, but my brother has been so attentive to her that there hasn't been much for us to do.

I find her a moment later, one hand propped against the wall for support.

I rush toward her. "Are you all right? Why are you out of bed?"

"I needed to go to the bathroom." She places her hand on her stomach. "And afterward I felt… I don't know. I just feel… I can't find Calder. Or my mom. I tried calling both of them, but neither one of them answered. I've already looked in his office, but he wasn't in there. And I can't—" Her face scrunches up in pain and she sucks in a ragged breath.

Oh, shit. "Are you having contractions?"

She meets my gaze, and though her eyes are steady, I can see the fear and uncertainty lurking in their depths. "I think so. I can't tell if this is just another false alarm or if…" She doesn't finish. "Have you seen Calder?"

I shake my head. "No, but I'll help you find him."

Ward has finally reached us. "No, I'll look. Lou, you stay with her. Take her back to bed."

Lily looks like she might argue, but I grab her before she can say a word.

"Come on," I say. "Calder will have a coronary if he sees you out of bed. Especially if you're having contractions. Where are they? And how far apart?" If she's going into labor, then maybe going back to bed won't help. Maybe we need to take her directly to the hospital.

Lily looks a little dazed. "I don't know how far apart they are. I haven't been counting. I wasn't sure what was going on at first, and then I was looking for Calder… I've only had a couple. I think."

I glance out a window as we pass down the hall. It's pouring outside. And thundering. I hope we find Calder quickly. The roads get pretty nasty out here when it storms, and there's a bridge on the way back to the main road that has a tendency to flood when the weather gets especially bad. Even if her contractions are still quite far apart, we should probably get her off the estate before we have to worry about getting stranded.

When we get back to her room, I help Lily into bed before reaching for my cell phone. I hit Calder's number. I don't know why he'd pick up for me if he isn't answering Lily's calls, but it's worth another try. We need to make a decision, and fast.

Surprisingly enough, he answers on the second ring.

"Louisa," he says, "now isn't a good time." In the background, wherever he is, I can hear the rain—and a car horn.

"Where the heck are you?" I demand.

"I'll explain everything later. I told you, now isn't a good time—"

"Lily's having contractions." I glance over at my sister-in-law, who's watching this exchange closely. I turn and take a couple of steps away from the bed. I need to remain calm. Keep Lily calm. And yelling at Calder isn't going to help.

But apparently I don't need to yell at him at all.

"She's in labor?" His voice is quiet, almost

disbelieving, but I detect a hint of fear.

"We don't know yet," I say. "That's why we were trying to find you. Where are you?" He's definitely not in the house.

"I'm in Barberville," he says.

"Barberville? In this weather?"

"It's a long story," he says. Then he sighs. "I've fucked up, Louisa."

My stomach tightens. "What do you mean?"

"Lily's mother is gone. She agreed to stay at a hotel here in town for the time being, but the moment my back was turned, she just left. All I have is a damn note."

"She what?" I never really warmed to Lily's mom, but I still don't want to believe she'd do this. "She's just gone?"

"She checked out of the hotel where I left her. I was going to try and catch her at the airport—"

"What's going on?" Lily says from the bed behind me. "Let me talk to him."

It's a fair enough request, since this concerns both her husband and her mom.

"Lily wants to talk to you," I tell my brother. "Why the heck didn't you pick up her calls?"

"I didn't want her to have to worry about any of this—at least not until I'd found Michelle."

"Well, it's too late for that." I glance back at Lily, who holds her hand out for the phone. The apprehension in her eyes is plain. She knows something is wrong, and hiding it from her isn't going to help. Calder owes her an explanation.

"I'm giving the phone to Lily," I tell my brother. He starts to argue, but I ignore him and pass the phone.

"Calder?" Lily says, her voice shaking slightly.

She's silent for a moment, listening. For a second, I wonder if he's going to lie to her or feed her some half-truth, but then her eyes widen.

"You did what?" she says. I can't tell from her tone whether she's angry or sad or afraid—probably a combination of all three. "Why did you do that? Where is she?"

Every second she's on the phone, her face gets paler, her eyes wider. This is definitely the last thing she needs right now.

"Why would you just leave her there?" she says. "Why didn't you tell me—" Her voice cuts off and she grimaces. A small sound of pain escapes her lips. We don't have time for this, not with the way she's reacting to these contractions. Not with the way the rain is coming down.

I grab the phone out of Lily's hand. "Calder, I'm taking her to the hospital. You guys can finish this conversation later."

"Is she all right?" I don't think I've ever heard my brother sound so distressed. "What's happening?" He doesn't even wait for my answer. "I'm heading back there right now."

"Meet us at the hospital."

Beside me, Lily is gripping the sheets with white knuckles, her face twisted in pain. We need to leave now.

"Has Lily—"

"Meet us at the hospital," I repeat. I glance out the window, out where the rain is coming down in sheets. If we don't leave now, we might never leave.

14

CALDER

Lily is in labor. *Lily is in labor.*

That thought drives out everything else—even the raw, gnawing feeling in my gut when I think about what Michelle has done—and suddenly nothing matters but getting to my wife.

If I was a madman on the road before, it's nothing to how I drive now. I don't care about the rain or the traffic. I don't care if a cop chases me down for driving twice the speed limit. I'm getting to that hospital. Getting to my wife.

I should have been there, I think. *I should have been by her side when this started.* But though the guilt eats away at me, I can't think about that now. I have one concern and one concern only—getting to her. Being with her as soon as humanly possible. Holding her hand as the pain comes. Even over the phone, I could hear the fear in her voice.

I need to be with her.
And if I have to kill myself to get to her, I will.

15
WARD

Keep it together, man. They're counting on you.

I hate that I have to remind myself of that, but this situation is affecting me more than it should. My heart is racing as I help Lily down the front steps to the driveway. Lou has gone to grab Ramona, which means I'm solely responsible for keeping Lily calm right now. It's a tall order, considering how much my mind is spinning. I care about Lily, sure, but this isn't my wife or my baby—so why have I gone into full fight-or-flight mode?

Because this reminds you of Lou's pregnancy, you idiot, I think. I still remember the look in her eyes when she realized she was going into labor—she's brave, my Lou, but even she was terrified at that moment. And I nearly puked up my guts on the way to the hospital. Neither of us had any idea what we were doing.

But if our past experience with the whole labor

thing has made me agitated and restless today, it seems to have had the opposite effect on Lou. She seemed impossibly calm when she told me that we needed to get to the hospital. And when I look back toward the front door and see that she's caught up with us, she gives me a reassuring nod as she brings Ramona down the steps toward the car.

Keep it together. You've got this.

The storm isn't helping. The rain beats down on us as I help Lily into the backseat, and the thunder terrifies Ramona. She's screaming as Lou straps her into her car seat. I hate that we have to take her out in this storm, but we have no choice. Lou buckles herself between Ramona and Lily as I slide into the front seat.

I hate driving in this weather. I can barely see ten feet in front of me, and there are too many precious things in the car with me. The water is already several inches deep on some parts of the road. Lou warned me that the road out to the estate could get rough during heavy rains, but bad storms are few and far between, and I've never had to drive to or from the estate in weather like this. Now I understand why she was in such a hurry to leave.

In the backseat, Lily lets out a groan. I glance in the rear-view mirror for a split second—just long enough to see Lou take Lily's hand. With her other hand, Lou continues to try to quiet Ramona.

"Don't worry," she says to Lily. "We still have plenty of time to get to the hospital. Your contractions are still about nine minutes apart."

Even though she's not talking to me, her soothing voice brings me some peace. *My angel.*

But Lily doesn't seem any calmer.

"I can't believe she'd just leave," Lily mutters to herself. "I can't believe he took her away without telling me."

Lou filled me in on some of the details of the situation before she went to grab Ramona. I can't believe it either—but then again, maybe I can. Everyone could see that Lily's mother was causing issues. If it had been Lou in that situation, I would have done everything in my power to fix it. I would've given my life to make things easier for her.

A branch falls from a tree above and slams against the hood of my car. Both Lou and Lily cry out, and Ramona screams even louder, but I don't stop. I don't even slow. We need to get to the hospital. I'll worry about my car later.

My hands tighten on the steering wheel. It's dark out here, and even my brights don't do much to light up the road in front of me. I can tell that the water is getting deeper, though, and that isn't good. The road goes over the creek just ahead, and if we're going to run into any trouble, it'll be along this stretch.

I slow down as we approach the bridge. The rain is thundering against the car, and out my window I can see the water rushing along the road beside us, tumbling over itself toward the creek. It's already too deep, and it's still getting deeper.

Shit. Shit shit shit. I urge the car forward slowly, but I can already tell the water is too high to drive through. The banks of the creek must have overflowed. We can't even see the bridge yet.

"What's going on?" Lou asks.

"The water's too high," I tell her, trying to keep my voice steady. "I can try to keep driving, but it's going to flood the engine. We'd just get stranded."

Now that I've stopped the car, I risk another look in the rear-view mirror. Lily and Lou have both gone still, and Ramona is still screaming and kicking her little feet in the air.

"It's too dangerous," I say, my voice so quiet that I wonder if they can even hear it above the rain and Ramona's wailing. "If we get stuck out here…" I don't need to go on.

"Then what are we going to do?" Lily says. I can tell that she's trying to stay calm, but it's clear she's anything but.

"We go back to the house," Lou says. "We call an emergency number from there."

"If we can't get through," Lily says, "then an ambulance won't be able to get through, either."

"We can't stay here," I say. "The water's only going to get higher." I peer out through the windshield. My headlights show nothing but an endless sheet of rain. "We can't drive through this water, which leaves us with three options. The first is to get out of the car and try to wade through the creek, which will probably be even more dangerous than driving—not to mention the fact that we're still several miles from town. Our second choice is to find a spot to park a little ways back and wait for an ambulance to get here." *And hope they can figure out a way across the water. And pray that Lily doesn't have the baby in the car in the meantime.* "Our third option is to go back to the house."

Ramona's shrieks are getting louder and shriller with every passing second, in spite of Lou's attempts to calm her. Lily has closed her eyes—in pain or in worry, I don't know—and thunder crashes overhead, so close that all of us jump.

"We can't stay here," Lou says. "Not with the storm on top of us like this. A tree could fall."

And the water is still getting higher. I nod. "I'm taking us back to the house."

We both glance at Lily, but her face has contorted in pain. She's gripping the handle on the door so hard that I'm afraid she's going to rip it right off.

Jesus, we're screwed.

Lou shoots a look at me, and I'm sure my expression reflects hers exactly—we need to get Lily somewhere safe. And fast. I shift the car into reverse and turn around, trying to avoid the streams of water rolling down the side of the road.

Forget screwed—we're completely fucked. This is our only option, but it's not going to be enough. It's not nearly enough.

Lily lets out a strangled cry of pain, and I try to ignore it and focus on the road. I also try to ignore Ramona's wailing—which has turned into heaving, gulping sobs. My poor little girl is terrified. And she isn't the only one—Lou might be putting on a brave face, but she's also afraid.

And fuck me, I'm terrified, too.

16
LILY

I need Calder.

God, I need him. I need him to hold me in his arms and tell me that everything is going to be okay.

This can't be happening. Not now. Not like this.

Please, Bubble. Just stay inside me a little longer. Let this be another false alarm.

This can't be happening.

This can't be happening.

This can't be happening.

I bite down on my lip as the pain intensifies, pulsing outward from my lower back. I try not to make any noise, try not to show any suffering, but I know from the way Lou's hand tightens on mine that I'm not doing a very good job.

Lou is doing the best she can to help, I know. But I want Calder. I *need* Calder.

I need him.

Need him.

Need...

Thunder crashes overhead, and I let out a yelp. Ward curses and swerves around something in the road. Ramona is screaming, and though her piercing cries stab right through my skull, I'm secretly glad I'm not the only one who is afraid.

Breathe. In and out. In and out. Just breathe. It'll stop. The pain will stop. You're not in labor. Not tonight. Not in this weather. Not without Calder. Bubble will just stay inside you a little longer. It's not time yet. I'm not in labor.

I'm not in labor.

I'M NOT IN LABOR.

There's a lump in my throat. Am I crying? I don't know. I don't seem to be aware of anything but the pain pulsing through my lower body. It's lasting longer this time than it did before.

This can't be happening.

I need Calder.

When the worst of the pain finally passes, I bend forward, fumbling around on the floor for my purse. I did bring my purse, didn't I? We rushed out of the house so fast...

"What do you need?" Lou asks.

"My phone," I say. "I need my phone..." *I need Calder...*

"Here, use mine." She presses her cell into my hand.

I don't waste a minute. I find Calder's number and call him. He answers on the first ring.

"Louisa?" Calder says. "How far are you? How's Lily? I'm at the hospital, and I told them to expect—"

"Calder."

He's silent for the space of a breath. Then, "Lily."

186

"Calder." This time, I can hear the panic in my own voice.

"Where are you?" he says. I can tell he's trying to keep his voice steady, but it isn't working. Hearing him like this makes it even harder to breathe.

"We're not going to make it to the hospital," I whisper.

"What?"

"We can't make it," I say. "The road has flooded. We can't get to town. We're heading back to the house."

He's silent for so long that for a terrible moment I'm afraid something has happened.

"Calder?"

"I'm coming to you."

Tears well up in my eyes, and for the first time in many weeks I don't care if I'm being overemotional. "You can't. The road—"

"I'm coming."

"But—"

"I'm coming to you. If I have to fight my way through hell, Lily, I swear I will do it."

He can't. It's not safe. And even if he tries, he'll never make it…

"It might be another false alarm," I whisper.

"I don't care. I'm coming."

In the background, I hear the screech of his tires on the wet asphalt. I swear, if he gets himself killed…

"Calder, please don't—" My voice cuts off as my body tenses. Even though I'm between contractions, my lower back still hurts.

"Lily?" Calder says, his voice rough.

"I'm okay," I tell him. "I'm okay, I promise. Just don't—"

Ward's car suddenly starts shaking violently.

"What's going on?" Lou asks. Ward is cursing.

"Water must have gotten into the engine," he says.

Just as suddenly as the car started shaking, it stops—but so does the engine.

"Lily?" Calder says in my ear. "What's happening?"

We're at the gate to the estate, but the car doesn't seem to want to go any farther. Ward curses again and tries to restart the car, but nothing happens. We've completely stalled.

"Lily," Calder says again, more firmly this time. "Tell me what's happening."

"We're going to have to walk the rest of the way," Ward says.

"The car engine flooded," I tell Calder. "But we're at the gate. We're walking the rest of the way back." I push the car door open and am immediately hit with a wall of rain. "Calder, I need to hang up." I don't want to. I need his voice in my ear. I need him to tell me that it's all right, that he's coming to me. But right now I need to focus on getting back to the house.

"Call me back when you're inside," Calder says. "Promise me."

"I promise," I say, stepping out into the rain. "I love you."

"I love you, Lily. I'll be there as soon as I can."

"Be safe."

If he says anything, it's drowned out by a crash of thunder. And then Ward is in front of me, reaching down to help me out of the car. He hooks his arm around my waist, and though I almost argue that I don't need his help walking, I know that would be a lie. Lou has a still-screaming Ramona in her arms, and she's trying to protect the baby from the worst of the rain. Together, we start the trek up the long driveway.

I have another contraction on the way back to the house. I don't say anything, don't let myself stop. But I think Ward can tell, because his arm tightens on my waist.

When we finally get inside, I'm exhausted. We're all soaked from head to toe, and I desperately want to pour myself into some dry clothes and hide in my bed. But there's no time to change, no time to rest—I'm hardly in the door before another contraction hits, and I nearly double over as I try to fight it.

Please, Bubble. Just hang on.

We don't bother trying to make it up the stairs. Instead, Ward leads me into the front parlor and helps me down onto the sofa.

It's going to be all right, I tell myself. *I can do this. Everything will be fine.* But it's hard to make myself believe that. Ward and Lou have been great—more than great—but they aren't Calder. I want him here so much that it hurts.

Everything hurts.

My chest is tight. My heart is beating too fast and too hard. I don't know what I'm doing. I'm not ready for this.

Not ready.

Not ready.

Not ready.

I can't have this baby. Not like this. Not without Calder.

"I need a phone," I say.

This time it's Ward who passes over his cell. I call Calder. He answers immediately.

"Lily."

"Yes," I say breathlessly. "We're in the house."

"The baby?"

"We're okay." I lay my hand on my belly as I lean back against the pillows. "I've still got a few minutes between contractions. I think." My mind is overflowing. I read every pregnancy book I could find over the last few months, did everything I could to prepare myself for this moment—but I'm not prepared. I can't seem to remember what I'm supposed to do now. I always assumed I'd be at a hospital when it came to this part.

"I'm ten minutes away," Calder says.

My stomach tightens. "Be careful. Maybe I should hang up—"

"I'm using my ear piece. Both of my hands are on the wheel, I promise."

"Calder, you should—"

"I'm not hanging up, Lily."

I close my eyes. I know I should continue to insist that he hang up, but I can't find the strength.

"I'm so scared," I whisper. Now that I've admitted it out loud, the panic is rising in my throat again. "Calder…"

"Breathe," he says. "You can do this, Lily."

"I need you."

"I'll be there soon."

But it doesn't matter when he gets here—we'll still be stuck here, at the estate.

"I can't do this," I hear myself say. I'm half-delirious with fear. "Not like this. Not like this, Calder. I can't. I'm supposed to be in a hospital. I'm supposed to have doctors and nurses and—"

"You can do this," he says again. "And you will. You're strong, and you can do this."

My hands are shaking, but I'm not sure whether that's from the fear or from the cold that has started to settle into my bones. While I've been talking to Calder, Lou and Ward have been rushing around, and now Ward comes toward me with a blanket.

As he wraps it around me, my next contraction starts. I bite down a groan.

"Stay with me, Lily," Calder says in my ear. "Stay with me."

"I'm... here..." I say.

"I'm almost there," he says. "I'm almost to the bridge."

"Be careful," I tell him through gritted teeth. "I swear, if you do anything reckless I'm going to kill you."

"You only have one job," he says. "Focus on the baby."

"I know, but—"

"Focus on Bubble, Lily. And breathe."

How am I supposed to breathe right now? How am I supposed to think? How am I supposed to do *anything*? I'm stranded. Having a baby. And my husband is out there in a horrible storm and probably driving too fast and—

"I'm almost there, Lily," he says into the phone. "I'm almost there. Just hold on a little longer."

A little longer. Just a little longer.

"Calder," I say, "I—"

A crash of thunder cuts me off.

And Calder curses in my ear.

"SHIT!"

"Calder?" I say, sitting up. The blanket falls from my shoulders. "Calder, what—"

On the other end of the line, I hear the screech of

tires—then the deafening and unmistakable sound of crushing metal.

And then the line goes dead.

17
LOU

Lily's face has gone white.

"Calder?" she says into the phone, her voice cracking. "Calder! Calder, answer me!" Her hand visibly shakes as she pulls the phone away from her ear.

"What's going on?" I ask her, running over and shifting Ramona in my arms. I've just managed to get my little girl to stop crying. "What happened?"

She doesn't answer. Instead she hits a couple of buttons on the screen, presumably calling him again. I glance over at Ward, but he looks just as shocked and confused as I feel.

After a moment, Lily drops the phone, her eyes wide with horror.

"What happened?" I ask again, my stomach sinking further with every passing second. Something is wrong. Something is desperately wrong. Ramona starts to whimper in my arms.

"Lily," Ward says firmly. "You have to tell us what's happening."

Lily glances up, blinking, as if she's suddenly remembered she's not alone.

"Something happened," she whispers. "Something happened to Calder."

She's in shock, that much is clear. The bottom falls out of my stomach.

"I'm sure he's all right," I hear myself tell her. "He'll be here soon."

But Lily is shaking her head. "No, no… no, he's not all right. He's not all right. He's—" She winces and grips the arm of the couch as she has another contraction.

I glance back at Ward, and his expression doesn't reassure me. He has a look on his face that I've only seen a handful of times in my life—and I know we both sense that this night is about to get a lot worse.

"Lily," I say when her contraction has passed. "Lily, what happened?"

Ramona starts to cry in earnest again, and I bounce her on my hip, but it's hard to concentrate on anything until I hear what happened to my brother.

"I think… I think there was a crash," Lily says. "There was a horrible sound, and he… he's not answering, and I…"

"I'm sure he'll call you back when he can," I say. "He's probably dealing with the other driver now. And calling the cops. And dealing with all of that stuff."

But she keeps shaking her head. "There aren't any other drivers. He said he was almost to the bridge. It was just him. If he's… If he…"

I don't even want to think about that. *My brother is fine. My brother is fine. My brother is fine.* If I think it enough times, maybe I'll start to believe it. I can't afford to panic right now.

I look over at Ward again, and he's watching me with a look in his eyes that I can't name. Ward and Calder aren't exactly best friends yet, but I can tell this news is affecting him as much as it's affecting me and Lily.

And then suddenly he goes over to Lily, picks up his phone, and then turns and walks toward the door.

"I'm going to go get him," he says over his shoulder.

Wait—what?

I hurry after him. "Ward!"

He pauses at the doorway, waiting for me to catch up to him. Ramona has gone back to whimpering, and Ward's eyes soften slightly as he looks down at her.

"The road is underwater," I remind him.

"I'll drive until the water is too deep and then get out and walk. Or swim."

"Your car—"

"I'll take yours."

It's clear he's thought this through, but I'm torn. On the one hand, my brother is out there. Possibly hurt. Possibly worse—*but I won't think about that.* We need to do whatever we can to help him.

On the other hand, the idea of Ward going out there in this weather, with the storm on top of us and flash floods rising with every passing moment... it makes me sick to think of it. And he wants to *swim* through it? No way. No, no way. If anything happened to him...

He touches my cheek. "I'll be careful, Lou, I promise." He glances over my shoulder. "We need to be strong for them right now. I'll go find Calder. You need to stay here and help Lily. I've got my phone if anything happens, but you should call nine-one-one. They'll tell you how to help Lily."

Curse him, he's right. I nod, but my heart aches.

"Don't do anything stupid," I tell him.

"I won't. And I'll bring your brother back." He reaches down to Ramona, who quiets a little at his touch. One side of his mouth curls up, and he leans down to kiss our daughter on the forehead before looking back up at me.

"I love you," I whisper.

"I love you, too." He tugs me toward him and kisses me fiercely—so fiercely that it makes my fear come back in a rush—before releasing me.

And then, without another word, he's gone.

18
LILY

I don't know which is worse—the fear or the pain.

My earlier contractions were uncomfortable, but now... now I don't know what to do.

And Calder...

Calder...

My throat aches.

My eyes ache.

I want to scream. To sob.

But I can't seem to do anything at all.

And then another contraction comes, swelling through me, and I'm lost in the panic and the pain again.

Please, Bubble. Please wait. It isn't time yet.

"Lily."

That's Lou's voice, and when I open my eyes, she's kneeling beside me.

"Ward has gone to get Calder," she says. She tries

to smile at me, but I can tell she's just as scared as I am. Still, her words soothe me a little. Ward will get Calder. If Calder is still...

Lou squeezes my hand. She's put Ramona down somewhere—I can hear the poor little thing crying—and guilt washes through me.

"Ramona..." I say.

"She's in her playpen. She can tell something is going on. But she'll be all right." Lou gives another attempt at a smile. "Lily, can you tell me where your cell phone is? I ran up to your room to look for it, but I couldn't find it anywhere."

My cell phone? I remember using it to call Calder earlier today, but I have no idea what I did with it after my contractions started. And I'm having trouble thinking of anything through my panic. "I... I don't know."

"That's all right," she says, giving my fingers another squeeze. "Do you remember what you did with mine? Did you bring it in with you, or is it still out in Ward's car?"

I feel like I'm suffocating. "I-I don't know." I remember hanging up on Calder. Stumbling through the rain with Ward's arm around me. Fighting back pain and fear. But I have no idea what I did with that phone.

Lou's face is impassive. "I think I might need to go look for it. I have to call nine-one-one."

I don't want her to go. The thought of being alone in this house while everyone else I love is out in the storm makes me want to sob. But I know we have no other choice.

"Okay," I tell her.

"I'll be quick," she promises. "Just tell Bubble to

hold on. You're going to be okay, Lily. We're going to get through this."

I lean my head back against the pillows. "You don't have to do this, Lou."

"Do what?"

"Pretend that everything's okay. Put on a brave face for me." I tighten my grip on her hand. "We both know that none of this is okay. That we're fucked. That this is all fucked." Somehow, just admitting that out loud gives me a little more strength. "I'm having a baby in the middle of a storm and Calder is out there somewhere... And now you and Ward are putting yourselves in danger to help. None of this is okay. But I guess we don't have any choice but to push through."

Lou gives a single nod but doesn't say a word.

"We've got to push through," I repeat, and I'm not sure whether I'm speaking to myself or to her. Somehow, we've got to survive this.

But God, I don't know how.

19

WARD

The rain is coming down so hard I can't see more than two feet in front of me. It slams against me, and I duck my head, pushing forward. The water is already ankle-deep in most places, and higher than that in others.

I had to abandon Lou's car earlier than I'd hoped. I didn't realize the road would get so bad so fast. It's rained plenty of times since I've started living at the estate, but we've never had flooding like this—and now I'm cursing at myself for not preparing for this possibility. Lou told me it was a risk, but I spent all my time and energy renovating the house when I should have dealt with the bridge. And now everything is at stake.

Lou...

All I can think about is the look in her eyes when she realized her brother was in danger. I want to help

Calder, yes, and I'm worried for Lily, of course... but it's Lou's eyes that I see in my mind. It's her terror that I feel deep in my bones. She's the reason I'm out here.

She'd kill me if I let anything happen to Calder. And I'd kill myself if my own carelessness got him hurt. I should have known better. Should have fixed the road...

Thunder crashes overhead, and I keep my head down. The water is getting higher—in the deeper places, it's up to my knees now, and it rushes around my legs, carrying branches and other bits of debris down the road. I have the flashlight from Lou's glove compartment, but the light doesn't help much. I still can't see anything. I'm not even sure I'm still on the road.

But I have to get to Calder. To find him and bring him back safely to his wife and his sister.

For Lou. Always for Lou.

I don't care if it takes all night. I will find him.

20

CALDER

I've got a headache that threatens to rip my skull apart.

For a moment, that's all I know—the pain shooting through my temples. And then, little by little, I become aware of another pain, this one in my left leg. And then yet another pain in my back. My ears are pounding.

And am I wet?

I sit up—which is much more work than it should be—and my entire body aches with the effort. My head is throbbing, and when I blink, everything around me is dark.

I rub my eyes, and even that is a little painful. It takes a moment for my vision to focus, and when it does, I find myself staring at a bunch of leaves.

I'm in a fucking tree.

But no, that can't be right—I don't remember how

I got here, but even dazed as I am, I know it's impossible for me to be in a tree. And yet there's a branch in front of my face. And leaves all around me. A raindrop slides off of one of the leaves and lands on my cheek. The wetness feels real, and I'm in too much pain to be dreaming. So where am I, and how the hell did I get here?

The air tastes thick. Powdery, almost. Or are those specks floating in front of my eyes just a figment of my frazzled brain?

I feel around me. I might be in a tree, but I also appear to be in a chair of some kind. No, wait—a car. I'm in a car.

And that powder in the air is from the airbag.

My air bag deployed. I must have been in a wreck.

Suddenly it all comes rushing back—the storm, the flood, the need to get back to the estate. I was driving way too fast, doing everything in my power to get to Lily.

Lily. Lily is in labor. Lily is stranded at the estate. Lily needs me. Suddenly my pain doesn't seem to matter anymore—I have to get to her.

It takes me three tries to get my door open. When I finally climb out into the rain, I see why—there's a tree across the front of my car. It fell across the road, landing on my hood and completely crushing the front end of my car. If I'd been a foot farther down the road, it might have killed me.

But I don't have time to stand here and consider that morbid revelation. I have to get to Lily.

I twist around. The water is high on the road, but that doesn't matter. I can swim if I have to. Nothing will keep me from Lily.

It takes me a moment to get my bearings—I know

this place well, but between the weather and the pulsing beat in my skull, it's nearly impossible to tell one direction from another—but I finally set off toward the house.

The water gets higher with every step. It rushes around my legs, whipping branches and leaves and other debris along past me. The rain pounds against my skin, and every flash of lightning sends another stab of pain through my head. My left leg twinges with every step, and now that I'm walking, I can tell that something might be wrong with my back as well. But no ache or pain will keep me away from Lily a moment longer.

Lily...

She's in labor. Stranded at the house. Without me. How did this happen? How did I end up away from her at a time like this?

But I know the answer to that, and I only have myself to blame. Just thinking of her mother makes me sick to my stomach—but I'd endure that shame a hundred times over if it meant I could be next to Lily right now. I swear, if anything happens to her...

A branch crashes down into the water next to me, but I don't even flinch. I keep pressing forward, even though the flood is now up to my knees and moving so fast that I can feel it trying to push me off my feet.

I don't care if this is dangerous. I need to get to Lily. No matter what. She must be so scared. She might be—

Just get to her, you fool. Get to her as quickly as possible. Get there, even if it kills you.

And as I push forward through the storm, I realize *that* is a very real possibility.

21
LOU

Just stay calm.
Just stay calm.
Just stay calm.

It doesn't matter how many times I say it to myself—it gets harder with every passing second. I spend almost twenty minutes searching for my cell phone in the rain, but I can't find it anywhere. It's not in the car. It's not on the driveway. It's just gone. Finally, I force myself to give up the search and return to check on Lily—and I'm not a moment too soon.

If I had any hope that we might make it through the night without this baby—after all, I was in labor for nineteen hours—it's fading fast. After five minutes at Lily's side, it's clear that her little one has no intention of waiting for help to arrive, and she seems to know it, too. Even if I thought I still had a chance of finding my cell phone, I can't leave Lily now.

Both Ward and Calder are still out there somewhere. It's just me and Lily—and a whimpering Ramona, who's still clearly confused and terrified. I long to go over to my daughter, to pick her up and hold her close and promise her that everything will be all right, but I'm needed here.

I wipe Lily's forehead.

"Just keep breathing," I tell her. "Take deep breaths."

She nods. "I'm trying." Her voice is strained, but she forces a smile. We're both still trying to be strong for each other—and though I'm sure it's as easy for her to see through my bravado as it is for me to see through hers, I'm still grateful for the game. Maybe if we both fake it long enough, we'll start to feel it.

We got her out of her wet clothes, so now she's naked beneath the blankets. Her contractions are currently about three or four minutes apart, and they seem to last forever. I keep trying to remember how things went when I was in labor—I've been through this before, I should know what to do—but it's harder than it should be. Did the doctor have me start pushing at three minutes? Two? How the heck am I supposed to know if she's dilated enough? What am I supposed to do with the baby after that? What if there's some sort of complication? Are we sure the baby is pointed in the right direction?

I try not to overthink it, but that's next to impossible.

Lily's hand tightens on mine. Her teeth grind together, and I know this contraction is a bad one. But she doesn't say a word. Hardly even makes a sound.

We'll get through this, she and I. Somehow.

22

CALDER

I have to swim.

The current is so strong that it keeps knocking my legs out from under me. I'm soaked. My whole body aches. But I can't stop. Not here, not now.

Lily.

I gasp as the water slams something hard into my side, knocking me over. Water sweeps over my head and into my nose and mouth. For a moment, I don't know which way is up. The flood is dragging me under.

And then somehow my feet find the ground again, and I fight my way back upright.

The water is around my waist. The thing that hit me is pushed into me again—it looks like half a fucking tree—but this time, I'm a little more prepared. I lunge out of the way and grab the trunk of a tree that's still rooted to the ground.

My chest heaves. If I'm not careful, I'll be drowned. But there's no time.

I need to get to Lily.

I release the tree and push back into the water. Yes, it looks like swimming is my only chance—I need to stop fighting the rushing water.

It's a foolhardy plan, but I don't care. I need to get to Lily as soon as possible. I'll take any risk. Endure any danger.

At the last moment before launching myself into the current, I pause to peel off my outer layer of clothes and my shoes. I can't have them weighing me down.

And then I dive into the water, praying this isn't where I die.

23

WARD

I can't see a damn thing.

The rain is coming down too hard, and I've accepted that this flashlight is completely useless. The water sweeps by me, and though I know it'll be impossible for anyone to hear me over this weather, I keep calling anyway.

"Calder!" I yell against the wind. "Calder!"

I'm almost to the creek. I've still seen no sign of Calder or his car, and I'm not sure whether that's a good or a bad thing. Even if I find him, it might be too late—but I won't get anywhere thinking like that. I need to keep going until I know one way or the other.

Lou's face floats into my mind—and Ramona's, too. It's the thought of them that keeps me putting one foot in front of the other, that keeps me pushing through the storm.

"Calder!" I shout again. But the words are carried away by the wind.

The water is at my knees. I look into the trees on either side of me, but there's no higher ground anywhere. I need to keep going. I need—

My flashlight pauses, then sweeps back over the water. I could have sworn I saw something... something that didn't look like debris...

There! It's unmistakably a human form. Unmistakably a man.

A man facedown in the water.

Shit. I charge through the flood, noticing too late that the water is faster and higher over here. I have to get to that man. Have to make sure it isn't Calder.

But I know it's him. I know it without seeing his face. I swear, if he's dead... Lou's face rises in my mind again, but I can't let myself think of her right now. I can't think about what I'll say to her if the worst has happened.

I'm nearly there. But the water is so fast, the current so strong, the rain so blinding, I'm not sure I'm going to make it.

Just when I'm starting to think I'll never reach him, that the flood will sweep him away, I see my chance. I lunge forward, grabbing him before the current can carry him off completely.

And immediately, a fist slams into my face.

I stumble back, falling ass-first into the swirling flood. Water sweeps over my head and the flashlight is torn out of my hand.

As I try to find my footing, a hand closes around my arm, yanking me back to my feet. I don't need any light to see who's standing in front of me.

"What the hell was that?" I demand. My jaw is

throbbing. "What the fuck, man?"

"What the hell are you doing out here?" Calder shouts over the rain.

"What do you think? Looking for your sorry ass." *And this is how you repay me.* I rub my sore face.

Calder doesn't say anything at first, and I hope he's feeling a good amount of shame right now.

"I thought you were a tree," he says finally.

"Do you usually punch trees?"

"When I'm swimming my way through a fucking flood, I'll do whatever it takes." He pauses for half a second. "Is Lily—"

"She was all right when I left her," I say. "But she'll be better when she sees you alive and well."

Another pause. "She thinks I'm—"

"We had no fucking clue what happened to you," I say. "Or do you think I'm out here for fun?"

He doesn't say anything. Instead, he turns and trudges through the water in the direction of the house. I hurry after him.

"What happened?" I ask.

"A tree fell on my car."

"Shit." I push my wet hair back out of my eyes. "How the fuck are you even walking right now?"

"I don't know. But I'm not going to stop until I'm with Lily."

I don't blame him. I'd do the same for Lou. *Lou... We'll be there soon, my angel. I promise.*

24

LILY

I can't do this. Oh, God. I can't.

I can't.

I can't.

I can't.

Not now. Not like this.

Lou's hand is clammy in mine. Or is it my hand that's clammy? I don't know anymore.

"Breathe," she tells me. "Just like you learned." She mimics the special breathing pattern I'm supposed to be using, but I can't concentrate on getting it right. I can't. I can't...

I'm not ready for the next contraction. They're coming so frequently now that it feels like they never stop, and they last so long that I'm afraid they're going to tear me apart.

I hear myself cry out in pain.

God, it hurts

it hurts
it hurts
it can't be happening like this
it hurts…

I'm not ready. My baby… my little boy… this isn't safe for him… he needs a hospital and doctors and nurses and… oh, God, I can't do this here. What if something happens? What if…

The pain intensifies, and I moan again. Everything is pain and heat and I'm sweating everywhere and between my legs I feel…

Not here, Bubble. Please. Please. Please.

"Lily," I hear Lou say from far away. There's a tiny quake in her voice—or maybe the room is just shaking.

Nothing feels right.

"Lily," Lou says a little louder, "I think you're going to need to push now."

No. Not now. Not here. I can't do this.

Calder isn't here. Calder might be… he might be… Does any of this even matter if he's gone? If something happened to him, I don't want to go on. I don't want to. Can't. I can't…

"*Lily,*" Lou says. "I need you to push."

No no no no no. I can't breathe. I can't do this. I just want to submit to the pain and float away. Just float away…

But Bubble needs you, a voice says in my head. *He's ready to be here in this world…*

A world without his father? Oh, God, if he never gets to know the man who made him, the best man I've ever known….

But I can't think like that. Calder will never forgive me if I give up now. Wherever he is. I need to do this for both of them.

In the distance, through the pain, I can still hear Lou's voice. And I push.

And push.

And cry.

And push.

And try not to think about Calder.

And push.

And scream.

And push.

And suddenly, somehow, it becomes easier. And Lou is saying something...

And a baby is crying.

He's here. Oh, God... he's here.

My body falls back against the pillows on the sofa. And just when I think I can't take anymore, I hear a voice calling for me.

Calder's voice. *Calder...*

But before I can answer, everything around me goes black.

25
CALDER

There's blood everywhere.

For a moment, that's all I can see. Blood all over the sofa. All over Lily. All over the baby...

Baby...

Lou has blood on her, too, but at least I know it's not hers. She has the baby—my baby—in her arms. And Lily...

Lily's eyes are closed. And she's so still. Too still.

I don't remember moving. But I'm suddenly at her side, gripping her hand, calling her name.

But she's not moving, not moving....

26
LILY

TWO DAYS LATER

They won't tell me what happened.

I remember the pain. The screaming. The fear.

I remember hearing the first, sweet cry from my son's throat.

I remember the miracle of Calder's voice, the proof that he was alive.

But after that, there's only darkness.

I woke up yesterday morning in the hospital. Calder tells me they were able to get an air ambulance out to us at the estate, but he won't give me any more details than that about what happened two nights ago after he made it to the house. And there's a desperate, hollow look in his eyes when I ask, so I don't press him for details.

Honestly? I'm not sure I want to know.

And truthfully, it doesn't matter. Calder is alive.

I'm alive. And our son is here. So much has happened in the past couple of days, and none of it feels real.

I look down at the tiny little human in my arms. He's perfect. Even though he arrived a couple of weeks before his due date, he's still round and healthy. He emerged with a thick crown of dark hair, and his eyes are a dark gray. He has all of his fingers and toes—I've counted them multiple times—and he has the softest skin and the sweetest smell and he's everything I ever could have hoped he would be.

He's sleeping now. And somehow it's the most fascinating thing in all the world.

The door swings open, and Calder stands there, a bag in his hand. For a moment, he just stares at us, almost as if he can't quite believe what he's seeing. And then he breaks into a wide smile.

"I brought you a cheeseburger from the cafeteria," he says, raising the bag.

My stomach gurgles in response—I'm starving, and that sounds perfect.

"Thank you." I look back down at the bundle in my arms. I don't want to take my eyes off of him. "He just went back to sleep."

Calder approaches the bed. I shift slightly, trying to give him room to sit without waking our son. He settles softly down beside me, wincing slightly as he slides his arm around me.

"You really need to go get yourself checked out," I tell him. After a lot of begging, I got him to tell me what happened to him and his car on the night I gave birth. I still can't believe he walked away from that accident, let alone swam through the flood. And of course, stubborn fool that he is, he's now refusing to let any of the doctors have a look at him. He refuses to spend any more than a few minutes away from my side.

"I'm all right," he tells me. "It's just a few bruises."

"It might not be—"

"I'm not leaving you," he says. "And that's final, Lily." He tightens his hold on me and pulls me back against his shoulder.

I don't argue. Honestly, I want him here with me. I thought I'd lost him. Now every moment together feels unspeakably precious—especially now that our son is here, too.

"I can't stop staring at him," I whisper.

Calder reaches over and sweeps his thumb gently against the little one's cheek. "He's got your nose."

I smile. "And your hair."

"And your chin."

"And your mouth." My grin widens. "I haven't decided whose ears he has yet."

A chuckle rumbles through Calder's chest. "Let's hope he got your ears."

"There's only one thing he needs," I say. "A name." As much as I'd like to keep calling him Bubble forever, I'm not that cruel. The time has finally come for us to make a decision.

Calder doesn't say anything for a long moment, and then he turns his head and brushes his lips against my cheek.

"You did all the work," he says. "You should pick his name."

"I didn't do *all* the work," I insist. "If it weren't for you, I would have—"

"Probably given birth here in the hospital, rather than scared and alone in our parlor."

His bluntness startles me—though it's clear he

went through hell that night, this is the first time I've heard him blame himself.

"That's not true," I tell him. "It's not your fault the bridge flooded. You're a hardheaded man, Calder, but even you can't control the weather."

"I couldn't have stopped the flood, but I could have been there when your labor started. Or at the very least, I could have picked up when you called me. If I'd known what was going on a little earlier, I might have made it back in time."

"You did everything in your power to get to me," I say. "You put your life at risk. You might have died out there." Even just admitting that out loud makes me shiver. The anguish of that night is still too fresh. "I thought I'd lost you."

His arm tightens around me. "I thought I'd lost *you*. God, Lily, when I saw all that blood..." He swallows. "I should never have left the estate in the first place, not while you were on bed rest. I should have been there for you. Instead, I was too busy trying to fix the mess I'd made."

A couple of days ago, I might have still blamed him for the role he played in my mom's departure—or at least torn him a new one for deciding to move her into a hotel behind my back—but his actions seem like such a small thing now. He didn't put my mom on that plane. He tried to stop her.

"It wasn't your mess," I tell him. "My mom made her own choices." My gaze drifts back to my son. *I will never leave you. Never.* "I should have listened to you all along. You knew she would only hurt me again, and even though I knew deep down that you were right, I just couldn't let her go. I wanted so badly to believe she'd changed, and I refused to acknowledge the truth—even when it was right in front of my face."

"Lily, you should know—"

"Wait," I say. "I need to make things right between us. To apologize for how I've behaved. You were only looking out for me, and I just turned everything into a fight. I'm sorry, Calder. I'm sorry for being so blind and so emotional. For making the last few weeks so much harder than they needed to be."

"Actually," he says, "it's me who should apologize. Lily, there's something you should know."

Something about his tone makes me twist to look up into his face. "What?"

"There's more to the story with your mother than I told you the other night," he says, and his dark eyes soften slightly. "I believe she genuinely wanted to get to know you. To mend the wounds between you."

I can't believe that now, after she's walked out on me a second time, he's suddenly changing his tune about her. That he's actually coming to her defense. "I don't understand."

"She was keeping a secret from us, Lily. I only found out about it just before she left." His gaze searches mine, and I suspect he's trying to gauge whether or not I'm emotionally stable enough to hear what he's about to say. "She didn't want me to tell you, but I refuse to keep it a secret from you."

"What is it?" I ask, suddenly apprehensive. What could my mom have been hiding?

"She's sick," he says softly. "Dying, actually. She said it was cancer, but she didn't give me any of the details."

I feel like I've been hit by a truck. It takes me a full minute to find my voice.

"Cancer?" I finally croak. *My mom is dying?* So many emotions flood me at once that I have no idea what I'm supposed to feel.

Calder is frowning. "I shouldn't have said anything yet. I should have given you a few days—"

"No. I'm glad you told me." *Even if I'm feeling paralyzed right now.* "I just... Are you sure?"

"She might have been lying to me, but I don't think so." His fingers slide down my arm. "If she was planning to leave all along, why didn't she just take the money I offered her?"

We're going to have to talk about his little bribe attempt later, but I don't want to dwell on the subject right now.

"She left a note," he goes on. "But it was in my pocket in the storm, and God knows where those pants are now." Apparently he stripped down to his underclothes before attempting to swim his way back to the estate—but though I would have liked to see my mom's last message, his life means so much more to me. If he had to lose the note in order to get back to me safely, then I'm willing to live with that.

"It's all right," I say, bringing my attention back down to the baby in my arms.

"I can tell you what it said," he continues. "It said that her heart could be at ease, knowing we'd found each other. That she didn't want you to spend the next year focusing on death, but rather on the life you were bringing into this world."

Tears burn in my eyes. *God, will I ever regain control of my emotions?*

Even though I longed for her love, it was easy to hate my mom. To think of her as selfish and flighty. To be annoyed by her probing questions and tactless comments. But now I see her as a confused, vulnerable woman only trying to make things right when faced with the prospect of her death.

"It's not fair," I whisper. After all this time, we could have fixed things. We could have had *some* time together. "We should try to find her. She shouldn't have to deal with this alone."

"Lily, I don't think she wants to be found."

On top of everything else, this is too much. I pull my son in closer. *She could have been here. She could have met her grandson. We could have done something—helped her pay for treatment, or supported her after surgery, or even just been there for her. Anything is better than this.* I feel so helpless. The thought of her being off somewhere by herself, of her dying alone somewhere across the ocean, makes my chest ache.

The little miracle in my arms shifts in his sleep. His tiny mouth opens slightly, but he doesn't make a sound.

You're needed here, I remind myself. *You have a life to nurture. It's your turn to be a mother now, and you need to be here for your son.*

And I will. If I have to make a choice, then I will always choose my son.

In the meantime, though, I lean back against Calder and let the tears fall.

27

CALDER

I wait until both Lily and the baby are asleep before I decide to sneak out. As much as I want to sit here with her in my arms forever, our conversation about her mother reminded me of a call I need to make.

I look down at her before I leave. Her brown hair is in a messy bun on her head, and she doesn't have a stitch of makeup on, but I don't think I've ever seen her look so beautiful. I lean over and press a kiss against her forehead as I lift our sleeping son out of her arms.

He's so tiny that I'm afraid I'll break him. But even though he was born a little early, the doctor told us he's perfectly healthy—and after hearing him scream this morning, I'm tempted to believe him. This little guy has quite a pair of lungs on him.

I settle him gently in the bed the nurse wheeled in for him. I can see so much of Lily in him—and so much of myself. I knew I would love my son, but the intensity of my feelings is startling. When I think of how close I came to losing both of them, my entire body tenses.

My son. His eyelids flutter as he sleeps, and I give him a final touch on the cheek before stepping out of the room.

I haven't left the hospital since we arrived two days ago. I spent last night in a chair next to Lily's bed. My sister and Ward weren't able to come in the air ambulance with us that first night, but meanwhile, they've been handling everything at the estate. When the water lowered again late yesterday afternoon, they organized a tow truck to get my car. And they brought us some clothes and other supplies from home—including, by some miracle, my cell phone. Apparently they found it on the front seat of my car. The water wasn't high enough there to sweep it away, and the branches of the fallen tree must have protected it from the worst of the rain.

I had a handful of messages waiting for me on the phone—one from the credit card company, one from my work, and one from the private detective who I hired to look into Taran Harker. I ignored all but the last one.

The detective finally managed to locate Mr. Harker. He was even able to give me his new phone number. Though I've had plenty of other important things to think about these last two days, in the back of my mind, I've been mulling over what to do about this.

But the more time I spend with my new son, the clearer it becomes to me that there's only one course of action. And that conversation with Lily about her mom only solidified my decision. I pull up the number the investigator gave me and give it a call.

I clench and unclench my fist as the phone rings. My back aches—I know I'm going to need to see a doctor eventually—but there are more important things to do first.

Finally, just when I think my call is going to be ignored, someone picks up.

"Hello?"

His voice is familiar, even after a year. I clear my throat.

"Hello, Taran. This is Calder Cunningham."

"No," Taran says immediately. "No fucking way. I'm not having this convers—"

"Just hear me out," I say. "I know things started off on the wrong foot between us, but I want to make things right."

"Look, man. I don't want your charity," he says. "Why don't we just skip all the small talk and jump to the part where you have me arrested again?"

I don't blame him for being resentful about the way things played out before, but I remind myself that he handled things just as poorly as I did. I take a deep breath.

"I'm not offering charity," I say. "I'm just offering us both the chance to know the truth once and for all. I think we should take a DNA test."

He's silent for a long moment before answering. "I'm Wentworth Cunningham's son. I don't have any doubts about that."

"Then a DNA test will only prove it. And erase any doubts anyone else might have." Part of me still doesn't want to believe my father could have been unfaithful to my mother, but there's only one way to settle the question.

But apparently Taran is still thinking this over.

"What happens when the test reveals that we're brothers?" he asks.

"Then we figure out from there what we want to do, if anything." It might take us some time to move past how things started between us, but that doesn't mean we shouldn't try. I glance back through the window into the room where my wife and son are sleeping. Life is too short, too precious—and family is too important.

Taran is still silent.

"I'm not my father," I tell him. And Lily isn't her mother—but that doesn't mean our parents haven't shaped us into the people we are. Now we have the chance to do better than them, to be stronger. All of our family trials have led us to this moment. They've taught us how to be the best parents for our son.

"Okay," Taran says finally. "Let's do this."

* * *

A couple of hours later, Lily is awake again. I'm sitting at her bedside, watching our son sleep, when I hear her stir.

"Good afternoon," I say. "Feeling rested?"

"I could sleep for another ten hours," she admits. "But I'm not sure I can go another minute without holding our son."

I smile, rising. "Let me get him for you."

She props herself up against the pillow while I bring him over to her. He stirs in my arms, starting to wake, then lets out a tiny little wail.

"Hush," I say gently. "Don't worry. Here's your mother." I pass him down into Lily's arms.

She coos to him and rocks him gently, trying to

pacify him. But his wails only grow louder.

"He's probably hungry again," she says—and I detect a bit of anxiety in her voice. She's still getting the hang of nursing, and her last attempt didn't go so well.

"Do you want me to call the nurse?" I ask.

She shakes her head. "Let me try first."

It takes a little effort—and I can see her starting to get frustrated—but finally both mother and son seem to figure it out. She lets out a sigh and leans back against the pillow.

There's nothing quite as beautiful, quite as wondrous, as watching Lily nurse our son. And she seems just as enamored by the act as I am. She stares down at the child with all the love of the world in her eyes.

"I've thought of a name," she says finally. "What do you think of Noah?"

Noah. I look at him, getting a feel for the name, and the side of my mouth creeps up. "Because of the flood?"

"It's a little on the nose, I know," she says with a laugh. "But I've always liked the name. And though part of me just wants to forget the night he was born, another part of me wants to celebrate it. We survived it, Calder. We survived, and I've never felt more joy or more hope."

I sit down next to her on the bed, pulling her close. "I love it. I think it's the perfect name."

She strokes Noah's hair. His fingers curl against her breast in response.

"I have an idea for a middle name, too," she says. She looks up at me. "What do you think of Calder?"

"I…" The thought of giving our son my name

makes my chest swell with pride. I brush my lips against her temple. "I love it."

"Noah Calder Cunningham," she says softly. "I think it suits him."

It does. And there's never been a more precious child in all the world.

* * *

Later that afternoon, we have some visitors. Lou and Ward show up with Ramona, and their daughter seems fascinated by her new cousin.

"Ba!" she cries, reaching for him.

"Yes, it's a baby," Lou says to her. "His name is Noah."

"Ba ba ba," Ramona says. She looks so big next to Noah, and I pray that my son doesn't grow as quickly as my niece seems to. I'm not ready for that.

Honestly, I'm not sure I'm ready for fatherhood at all, but it's too late to worry about that now. Noah is here, and I'm going to love him and protect him as fiercely as I love and protect Lily.

I step back to give my sister room to sit down on the bed. While she coos over Noah, I go stand next to Ward.

"How does it feel to be a dad?" he asks me.

"It's indescribable," I say. It's still hard to believe that he's finally here. "It's... wonderful, of course. But also..."

"Absolutely terrifying? Yeah." He grins at me. "I'm warning you now—that feeling never really goes away."

"I can't imagine it would." I look over at my wife and my son. I'm going to spend the rest of my life protecting those two—and there's no job I want more in all the world.

"Don't worry, though," Ward continues. "A few things get easier. You'll get used to living on no sleep pretty quickly." He follows my gaze toward the bed. "And if you and Lily ever need any help with anything, you know you only have to ask."

"I appreciate that," I say sincerely. Ward and I didn't exactly get off to a great start—that seems to be a pattern with me—but I've come to respect him deeply. He's a good man—and the husband my younger sister deserves.

But I owe him more words than that.

"I never got a chance to properly thank you for the other night," I say. He risked his life to come find me in that storm, and I want him to know that I recognize that fact.

He just shrugs. "I know we've had our differences, but I wasn't about to let you drown. Besides, Lou would have killed me if I came back to her empty-handed." His grin widens as he rubs his jaw. "But you owe me for that punch, man."

"Yeah, I'm very sorry about that." I clasp his shoulder. "Why don't you let me get you a couple of drinks later to make up for it?"

"I wouldn't turn that down."

"Ward," Lou says from the bed. "Come look at what Noah's doing. It's adorable." She turns her smile toward me. "You did a good job with this little one, Calder."

"Don't look at me," I reply. "Lily is the one who did all the work." I meet my wife's gaze, and the smile she gives me takes my breath away.

Before she can say anything, though, our little family party gets even bigger.

"Is this a good time?" comes a familiar voice from

behind me. Lily's father has arrived with his fiancée in tow. He stopped by briefly yesterday, but this is Regina's first visit with the baby. She has several big "It's a Boy!" balloons with her.

"Dad!" Lily says with joy. "You're welcome in here whenever you wish. And Regina, it's so good to see you."

I stay by the door as Lily welcomes the new arrivals. Both Regina and David make a big fuss over Noah, and I'm grateful that, after everything that's happened with her mom, Lily has such supportive people in her life. Grateful that we all do.

Over the next half hour, there's much laughing and chatting and fussing over the baby. After a little while, Noah wakes up and starts whimpering.

"Here," I say, stepping toward the bed. "Let me have him for a while." I take my son into my arms and rock him gently.

For a moment, the rest of the room disappears. There's only me and Noah. My eyes soak up every inch of him.

My son. My little boy.

I look up, taking in the joyful smiles of the people around me.

My family.

Finally, my eyes find Lily's, and in her gaze I find all of the love I could ever need. Everything in my life—every pain, every struggle, every challenge—has led us to this moment, and I wouldn't trade any of it.

And as I look back down at Noah, as I think of all the new joys that await us over the coming years, I know that this is only the beginning.

EPILOGUE
LOU

TWO MONTHS LATER

Ward is loading the last of our luggage into the car when I emerge from the house with Ramona.

"Mama, burr!" she says as a sparrow flits by overhead. "Burr!"

"That's right," I tell her with a smile. "It's a bird. You're going to get to see a lot of those on our trip." I smooth back her curls as I walk down the steps to the front drive.

Ward pulls the trunk of the car closed and turns to us with a lopsided grin. "Are you ready?"

"What do you think, Ramona?" I ask her. "Are you ready for an adventure?"

It's taken us a couple of months to get the final details of our road trip worked out, but I don't mind so much—especially considering the new baby. Ward and I weren't about to run off at a time when Calder and Lily really needed our help, but now that they're starting to get the hang of the whole parenting thing, I can't wait to set off on this journey.

I hook Ramona into her car seat, and when I straighten again, my brother and Lily have come out of the house. Little Noah is sleeping in Lily's arms, and he's already grown so much in the two months he's been in this world. His dark hair keeps getting thicker and thicker, and he's starting to look exactly like Calder did in all of his baby pictures.

"Be safe," Lily says to me, leaning in for a one-armed hug. "I'll miss you."

We're only planning to be gone for three weeks, but that feels like a lifetime. Noah will probably have doubled in size by the time we get back.

"Make sure you're getting plenty of sleep," I tell her. "And promise me you won't work too hard." Lily has started resuming some of her work at the Frazer Center—but only part time, and only the things she can do from home. Both she and Calder have the wild-eyed, exhausted look of new parents, but they seem to be doing just fine. Maybe even better than fine. They might be tired and scared and overwhelmed, but I've never seen either of them smile more.

"And *you*," I say to the sleeping Noah. "You better go easy on your mom."

I turn to my brother next. We've never been particularly physically affectionate with each other, but for some reason, all of that awkwardness seems to melt away from me now. I grab him tightly in a hug, and he hugs me right back.

"Have a good trip," he tells me. "Try not to do anything too crazy."

"Me, crazy?" I grin as I pull away from him.

"Never."

"I mean it, Louisa," he says. "Stay safe. Don't do anything reckless."

"Just because you're older than me doesn't mean you get to lecture me," I tease.

"Family is always allowed to lecture." His tone is serious, but I see a glint of amusement in his eyes.

And maybe he's right—we're family, and that means looking out for each other no matter what.

Calder and I—along with our significant others—have some decisions to make in the coming months. Calder and Taran Harker each took a DNA test a little while ago, and the results finally came in last week. Once and for all, we know the truth—that Taran Harker is our half-brother. We have another sibling.

I'm still trying to process that news, but Calder and I both agreed that there was only one right course of action from here forward—to treat Taran like family. He has yet to take us up on our invitation to meet again, but that doesn't mean he might not change his mind. No matter what happens, we've made it clear that our arms are open. He's family, and family is a rare, precious thing.

I glance back over at Lily, who's giving Ward a hug. She hasn't been able to get in touch with her mom since that dramatic day that Noah was born, but she hasn't given up hope. And both her dad and her new step-mother have been extremely supportive—in fact, they're coming to stay at the estate for a couple of weeks to help out while Ward and I are gone.

Yes, we're going to make it, I think. Only a few years ago, both Calder and I each felt like we were alone in the world. But we've somehow managed to build ourselves a family again, and we seem to be welcoming new members to that family all the time. I've no doubt it will only continue to grow.

Tears of happiness burn in my eyes as I finally slide into the car to go. I wave to Calder and Lily as Ward goes around to the driver's seat.

"Ready?" he asks as he buckles himself in.

In response, I grab him by the shirt and yank him toward me, pulling him into a fierce kiss.

When I finally break away, his eyes are bright and he's grinning from ear to ear. "What was that for?"

"For everything," I tell him. "For my whole world."

We have a family, a home, a beautiful daughter, and a love that's deeper and more amazing than I ever imagined love could be. I'm thrilled to be going on another adventure with this man, but if there's one thing I've ever known to be true, it's this: that this life, this family, is the greatest adventure of all.

AUTHOR'S NOTE

I hope you enjoyed this final chapter of the Cunningham
Family's story!
I confess that I'm tearing up a little as I write this—I've had such
an incredible, emotional, and rewarding experience writing about
these guys, and I wanted to take a moment to thank everyone
who has taken this journey with me. I couldn't have done it
without your support.

While I don't have any plans to write more novels about the
Cunninghams, you might someday see a glimpse of them in
some of my other books (you might have noticed a couple of
references in this book to the Fontaines—I consider these series
to take place in the same story universe!), and I definitely haven't
written off the idea of releasing a few bonus short stories about
these guys for special occasions. ;)

In the meantime, though, know that in my head the
Cunninghams' journey goes on long after the final words of this
book, and I hope that their story lives on for you, too. To me,
their story has always been about more than the romance—it's
been about rising from the ashes of hardship and creating a life
full of beauty, love, and laughter. When you open your heart to
love, there's always hope.

xoxo,
Ember

P.S. If you're so inclined, please consider taking a moment to
leave a review. Even a couple of sentences can help new readers
find books they'll love!

BOOKS BY EMBER CASEY

The Cunningham Family
His Wicked Games
Truth or Dare
Sweet Victory
Her Wicked Heart
Take You Away
Lost and Found
Completely (short story)
Their Wicked Wedding
A Cunningham Christmas
Their Wicked Forever

The Fontaines
The Secret to Seduction
The Sweet Taste of Sin

The Devil's Set
Jackson

Want to be the first to know when Ember has a new
release?
Want exclusive extras and freebies?
Join Ember's newsletter!
(http://www.embercasey.com/newsletter.html)

ABOUT THE AUTHOR

Ember Casey is a twenty-something writer who lives in Atlanta, Georgia in a den of iniquity (or so she likes to tell people). When she's not writing steamy romances, you can find her whipping up baked goods (usually of the chocolate variety), traveling (her bucket list is infinite), or generally causing trouble (because somebody has to do it).

For more Ember Casey news, updates, and extras, check out http://embercasey.com. You can also reach her at ember.casey@gmail.com (she loves mail!) or join her new release list at http://www.embercasey.com/newsletter.html.

15858884R00143

Printed in Great Britain
by Amazon